# An Ocean Apart

美

## The Gold Mountain Diary
## of Chin Mei-ling

BY GILLIAN CHAN

Scholastic Canada Ltd.

*Vancouver, British Columbia,*
*1922*

美

## *Sunday, November 12, 1922*

I am very tired tonight, but this has been my best Canadian birthday. I finish it with time to write in you — my beautiful new diary.

I have never had a diary before. I didn't know what a diary was until Mr. Hughes explained it to me. I was very scared when he told me to stay behind at the end of school on Friday. I thought that he was angry. I thought he would shout at me, and make his moustache go all bristly like it does when he yells at Ivor Jones for pulling my pigtails. Bess had to push me to go up to his desk. She was going to stay, but Mr. Hughes waved her out of the classroom. It was all right because I knew she would wait for me. She makes me braver.

Mr. Hughes had a package in his hands which he gave to me. At first I did not understand, until he said it was a birthday present. This made my face get very red, especially when he said that I was the hardest working student he had ever had, that he couldn't believe how my English had improved so much in three years. He doesn't understand — no one does, except maybe Bess. I *have* to work hard. I am lucky to come to school, and I must learn all I can as fast as I can, so I can work too, and help my father earn the money we need to bring Ma and Little Brother to Canada.

I wanted to bring the present home and open it today, on my birthday, but Mr. Hughes made me open the package then, and there you were, Diary, so beautiful with your bright red cover. Mr. Hughes said that I was to use you to practise writing in. I thought that meant handwriting drills, and that maybe you were lovely to look at, but dull to use. But no, Mr. Hughes says I am to write in you my thoughts and feelings as well as what happens to me. This is a very strange thing to do, I think — who would be interested in what I, Chin Mei-ling, think, or what I do? When I told Bess all this on our walk home, she thought so too, but she also said that I was very lucky because Hughesy hadn't given her a present on her birthday. Declan liked my diary too.

Oh, this is so hard. I don't think I have done what Mr. Hughes wanted, Diary. I have only written about you, but I haven't written anything about what I did today, and it was such a good day. I will do better tomorrow, I promise. I must stop now because my hand is very crampy.

## Monday, November 13

It is very early, still dark. Baba left for the Baldwins' almost an hour ago. It takes a long time to get to Shaughnessy Heights and Mrs. Baldwin wants him there early to tend the furnace and cook breakfast. I think she's mean, but Baba says that I must not say that, as he is lucky to have a job with the Baldwins when so many people have no work at all. He says that we are both lucky that Mrs. Baldwin does not make him live at her house like the last houseboy did. It makes me scared to think about that. Even now, I see Baba so little. Sunday is the day I see him most — when he has the afternoon off. It is the best day of the week for me and yesterday was the most beautiful Sunday I have ever spent here.

I hope I am allowed to do this, write on one day the things I did on another day. You are a hard and confusing taskmaster, Diary!

Yesterday afternoon Baba and I walked by the sea and sat on the wall, looking at the grey waves. Baba loves the sea. I wonder whether he would have stayed on the land, or run away and become a fisherman if Uncle Wing-lok had not brought him to Canada? Baba looked very serious and he asked me how much I thought about Ma. This was a hard question, because I think about her a lot, but I did not want to make him sad for me, or to think that I was not happy to be here with him. Every day, was what I said, but I did not tell him that I thought of Ma many times each day. Baba smiled and said that he did too. He looked very hard at me, making sure our eyes saw each other. "I promise, Mei-ling," he said, "that we will do everything we can to bring your mother and brother here." He gripped my arm, so tight that it hurt. I knew that what Baba said was true. If we continue to work hard and save our money, we can pay their fares and their tax, just like Uncle Wing-lok did for us.

This was such a happy thought it made me smile.

I was waiting though, waiting for Baba to mention my birthday, but he didn't. I could not remind him. He just stood up and said that we had to hurry home. I felt a bit sad and disappointed. When I was little Ma would boil me an egg on my birthday and colour its shell red for good luck. I knew Baba had no time for such things that pleased small children, but I wanted him to say something. I was being foolish, but I still felt a little sad, so I thought about how you,

Diary, were my Canadian red egg. That helped.

My sadness turned out to be truly silliness. When we reached Pender Street, Baba would not let me go to our room. He insisted that we go to our restaurant. This was very strange, as he does not work there until six on his afternoon off. I said nothing, and when we got there I could still say nothing, but this was because I was so *surprised*. Wong Bak had cooked a special meal for me with all my favourite dishes, including *dong-goo jinggai* — I love the way the mushrooms' flavour goes into the chicken. Not only that, but my friends were there too: Tsung Sook, old Mr. Chee and Yook Jieh. I wish Bess could have been there too, but I know she would not be allowed to come to Chinatown.

So you see, Diary, why yesterday was so special!

## Tuesday, November 14

I do not like Ivor Jones. Is that a wicked thing to say? He is just a mean boy. I have never harmed him, but he tries to make me sad. He pulls my hair, dips the ends of my pigtails into the inkwell and sometimes pokes me with his pencil. Somehow he found out that Mr. Hughes gave me a birthday present of you, Diary. I do not know how. Bess swears she didn't tell him, and she would not lie to me. Now he keeps coming up behind me and yelling "Teacher's Pet" in my ear. He is very sneaky about this — he does not let Mr. Hughes or any other teacher see him.

In class I do not like to answer questions, but when Mr. Hughes calls on me I must answer him. When I do, Ivor makes noises, quietly so *I* can hear, but not Mr. Hughes. He sounds like he is slurping rice. I did not understand this, but Bess explained. Ivor is making that noise to show that he thinks I am sucking up (those are Bess's words, not mine) to Mr. Hughes. Why is he like this? Why is he so spiteful?

When school finished today, Ivor and four other boys were outside the door in the school-yard. Declan was with them. Bess looked at me as if to say that's how Ivor knew about you, Diary — you can't always trust little brothers. She made a face at Declan, but he would not look at her. The boys walked behind us, shouting things like, "Chinky, chinky Chinaman sitting on a fence, trying to make a dollar out of fifteen cents." They were very loud. People passing by saw and heard them but no one stopped them. I looked at the ground and walked as fast as I could. My cheeks were very hot and my heart was beating very fast. Bess's face had gone white and her lips were all tight. She stuck her nose in the air and told me to do the same, but I couldn't.

When Ivor ran forward and pushed me, Bess turned round, yelling back at him to go away.

He smiled that mean smile of his and asked her in a singsong voice if she was going to make him. Bess is very brave, but the other boys were coming up behind him. She stamped her foot at them. "Don't you threaten me, Ivor Jones. I've got a bigger brother than that worm, Declan. A big brother who will make mincemeat out of you!" Declan still wouldn't look at her when she said that.

Ivor just laughed and said that Bess's big brother wasn't here now, and pretended he was scared, shaking and covering his face with his hands.

Bess grabbed my hand and we ran. We didn't stop running until we reached the edge of Chinatown, and then we only stopped when we bumped into someone: a tall white lady with blond hair and a black suit. I waited for her to shout at us, but she didn't. She was looking over our heads to where Ivor and his friends were standing. In a very loud voice, she asked us whether the boys had been bothering us. She kept staring hard at them. I knew Bess was going to say that they had, so I kicked her ankle. It didn't hurt her, of course — I would never want to be as mean as Ivor, and besides, cloth shoes can't hurt much. Bess glared at me, but said nothing. The boys ran away.

I got very brave and apologized to the lady for running into her. To stop Bess saying what really happened, I told the lady we were just playing a chase game. I don't think she believed me. Bess said she had better go find Declan before he got into more mischief with Ivor. The lady looked as if she were going to ask questions, so I said goodbye quickly and hurried off without looking back. I have not seen her before — I wondered what she was doing in Chinatown. I liked her face; it was very kind.

## Wednesday, November 15

For the first time ever, I did not want to go to school today, all because of Ivor. Last night I kept waking up and seeing that nasty smile that he has. This morning my feet were very slow as I walked down Keefer Street to school.

I was nearly late, but this was good because I arrived just as the morning bell rang and the classes lined up to go in. Ivor was at the back of our line, but I did not have to stand near him because Bess waved me to the front to join her, and made Ada Howe move up to let me in, even though Ada grumbled.

In fact, all day Ivor left me alone; not once did he pull my hair or make silly noises. Maybe he is scared of Bess's brother. I have only seen Liam when he came to fetch Bess once when their mother was taken ill. Liam is huge. I would be scared of him.

Mr. Hughes gave us a dictation today. I found it much easier, perhaps because I have been practising writing in you, Diary! I could keep up and I think I spelled all the words right. Some people complained and wriggled on their benches, but Mr. Hughes said we should get used to dictations, especially if we wanted to take the high-school entrance examinations. Bess whispered that she didn't see any point to that, because she was not going to go to high school, no matter what Hughesy thought. I was shocked. That was not respectful. I would love to go to high school, but I know it will never happen. I will leave and find a job like Baba, maybe in one of the big stores downtown — wouldn't that be fine? I will wear a silk *cheong-sam* and sell beautiful Chinese silks and porcelain. In the evenings I will still work in our restaurant with Wong Bak, just like Baba and Tsung Sook do when their day work finishes. We will work very hard, and the money the restaurant earns will make all our dreams come true: Wong Bak will be able to retire and rest; Tsung Sook will have the money to go back to China and find a bride; Baba and me will bring Ma and Little Brother here and we will be a family at last. When we are all happy like this, I will not have time to be sad about high school.

Someone is knocking on the door, so I will stop. It sounds like Mr. Chee.

### *Later*

It was Mr. Chee. He had spent the day at Mr. Lee's store, drinking tea and playing *mah joong* in the back room. He was happy because he had won a little. He was also happy because he heard that letters had arrived from China and one was for us. I went to get it immediately and Mr. Chee insisted on coming with me. He walks slowly, but I do not mind because when he is with me the men on the street do not call out to me. I am lucky to have Mr. Chee looking out for me when Baba is working.

Mr. Chee does not get letters any more, so I could understand why he was excited about ours. Even so, I did not accept his offer to read it to me, although I so wanted to know how Ma is. It is too bad that I did not learn to read Chinese before I came here, and that Chinese school takes place when I must help Wong Bak get ready for the dinner hours. I will keep the letter safe in you, Diary, until Baba finishes work. Then he will read it to me.

### Thursday, November 16

I feel very sad today. My troubles with Ivor Jones are very little ones. Ma and Little Brother face far worse. Ma had got the village teacher to write for her. It was not good news. Baba's mother is not well. She has a griping pain in her side that never leaves her. It makes her weak and tired, so that Ma and Grandfather must do all the work on our land. Little Brother stays with Grandmother. The crop has not been plentiful.

Ma does not say it, but I would guess that

they have very little food. When he read this, Baba's face got very still, like it was carved from wood. I felt like crying, but held my tears back. They would have served no purpose. Ma asked if we could send some extra money to buy medicine. When I looked at Baba, he nodded. Then he sighed and I knew why. He was thinking how the extra money would mean that we could save less for the head tax and fare.

Baba has never told me exactly how much we have saved, but I know his dream is for both Ma and Little Brother to come together. When I think how much money we need, I feel very small. A thousand dollars and their fare on the boat — how many hours will we have to work for that? It seems so unfair that even a little boy must pay this. Baba says that we can do it, but only if we make the restaurant a success. I will work very hard. I shall swear by writing it down here, Diary, and I won't even think about high school. I will try and find other jobs too. I wonder if Mrs. Lee would pay me to help her in the mornings before I leave for school? And those men who spend their time smoking opium — Mr. Chee calls them opium ghosts — perhaps I could run errands for them. But Baba must never know if I do that. He says I am never to go near them.

### Friday, November 17

All last night I kept thinking about Ma and wishing I was there to help her. These thoughts made me determined, so I did something that will help, even if I am a long way away. Bess's bravery is rubbing off on me. I went to the Lees' store and asked them if they had work for me. Mr. Lee did not seem sure and I thought he was going to send me on my way, but then I spoke directly to Mrs. Lee, asking if I could help with the children in the mornings before school. She thought about it for what seemed like hours. Her eyes narrowed and I was sure she would say no. Then I had a wonderful idea. Mr. Lee always has to walk Lily to school because Mrs. Lee is so busy with the other children, and so tired because a new one is due very soon. He always looks *very* grumpy. I told Mrs. Lee that Lily could walk to and from school with me. She agreed at once. I am to come at seven in the morning and help dress the children and watch over them. It should not be too hard — they are all under six, apart from Lily. It will be big sister practice for when my brother comes. Mrs. Lee asked me how much I wanted to be paid for this. I did not know what to say, so I said the first number I thought of: 10¢. Mrs. Lee's eyes got narrow again and she wanted to know if this was for an hour. I quickly said that it was for each day. She accepted very quickly. Do you think I asked too little, Diary? I don't care if I did. It's still fifty cents a week that I would not have had before. I start on Monday.

It is late and my hand is tired, but I am going to write a little more today, Diary, because something funny happened at school.

Ivor Jones met his match.

Ivor only let me alone for two days. This morning he was back to his usual nasty self. I was in the schoolyard with Bess at recess, walking arm in arm and talking about the girl Liam is courting. Bess doesn't like her. We heard a rapping on the window above our head. It was Ivor, looking out from our classroom. He was being kept inside for being cheeky. But Mr. Hughes must have left the room, otherwise Ivor would still have been doing his lines. Instead he was pressing his face against the windowpane, so his nose was all flat. He was pulling his eyes into slits. Now he knew we were looking, he opened the window and started chanting "Chinky slant eyes" at me.

Bess told me to ignore him, which I did,

although his words did hurt. I bet Ivor wouldn't like it if I called him "Round eyes." Bess pulled me so I had my back to the window. Coming toward us was Sergeant-Major Bundy. I had forgotten that it was his day to be at our school for Physical Drill. I don't think Ivor saw him — he was too busy trying to make Bess and me turn around. He must have made a truly bad face, because the Sergeant-Major stopped and stared at the window. His face got very red and his eyes were glaring. He shouted, "Are you making faces at me, you little horror?"

Ivor went white and ducked below the windowsill.

Sergeant-Major Bundy looked at Bess and me. He said that we must tell him who the boy at the window was. Bess answered straight away with a huge smile, and told him Ivor's name and the room number of our class. Sergeant-Major Bundy ran off, his feet making the ground shake, and then making a great clattering noise in the school until he appeared in the window. He had hold of Ivor by the shoulder, and with his other hand he was hitting him with that funny leather stick he always carries. Ivor was howling, but Sergeant-Major Bundy didn't care. He kept repeating over and over that Ivor should show respect and not make faces.

I was very glad not to be Ivor then. Sergeant-Major Bundy always scares me. Bess told me that even some of the teachers are scared of him. I can see why. Bess was laughing, and I know, Diary, that I said what happened to Ivor was funny . . . but now that I have written it down, I can't laugh any more.

I have had you one whole week, Diary. It is nice to have a friend like you.

### Saturday, November 18

Sometimes I envy Bess. On Saturdays, her mother lets her sleep late, but for me it is big chores day. At least we have a window; some rooms don't. It is hard to push our mattresses through the window to hang in the fresh air after I shake them out. I clean and dust the room. It is so small that this does not take long. I am glad that we eat most of our meals at the restaurant, and do not have cooking mess in our room like some of the bachelors do. I get cross because the men do not always keep things clean. Bugs and mice come into our room too, no matter what I do! Then I think how it must be for those men, all alone, such a long way from home. Some of them are like us, saving to pay the tax and bring their family here, but others, like Mr. Chee, are old now — their families gone, or they are too old to work. My crossness goes a little and I feel sorry for them. At least my Baba and I have each other. But I still do not like bugs!

Today is also my day to help Mr. Chee. His room at the end of the corridor is tiny, just a little cubbyhole with room only for a bed and a chair. He laughs when I say that and asks me why would he need more room, as he has nothing to put in it. I take our bedding and his to the laundry and he walks with me. It is slow because he stops to talk to so many people, friends from the railway days. Mr. Lee's father worked with Mr. Chee, laying track through the big mountains — that is why he lets Mr. Chee stay all day in the back room of the store, drinking tea.

My chores went quickly today and my homework too, so the afternoon was mine. I went over to the Mahs' to see Yook Jieh. Sometimes Mrs. Mah will let Yook Jieh come out with me for an hour, if she has finished her work, but not today. Yook Jieh was working in the kitchen with their cook. There is to be a big banquet tonight at the Mahs' for their Clan association. It will be very grand. Mrs. Mah said I could visit quickly but not stay, as there was so much to do.

As soon as her back was turned, the cook sneaked little dumplings to Yook Jieh and me — shrimp dumplings — they were so good. He is a kind man, very jolly, with red cheeks like apples. He asked me if I would like to help tonight, maybe wash dishes. He said he would ask Mrs. Mah and she would pay me. I wanted to so badly. I've heard about these banquets, but girls like me do not get invited to them. Baba and Uncle Wing-lok used to go to them, but that was when Uncle was alive and things were good. I didn't know what to do — I couldn't ask Baba for permission. I thought quickly and said I would ask Wong Bak.

I ran all the way, and Wong Bak laughed at my red face and the way my words all tumbled out. He was cleaning *Oong choy*, washing the grit from the leaves. Tsung Sook was already there and he said he would stay and do my work. They are kind to me. Wong Bak said I was to watch the Mahs' cook closely and steal some recipes, as he is said to be the best in all of Chinatown.

I am so excited! A banquet — even if I am only in the kitchen.

Oh, Diary, I am so tired this morning. I did not get home until way past midnight. Baba was asleep already so I tiptoed in. The Mahs' cook walked me home. He said it was not safe or proper for a girl like me to walk alone at that time. He was shocked that my Baba did not fetch me. I told him my Baba had not known what I was doing. The cook made a humphing noise, and said I should not be thoughtless like this again. I felt very ashamed, because his words were true ones that lodged in my heart.

But it had been exciting! The banquet last night was like seeing another world. I must write it down, because I want to remember it when I am an old, old lady — surely I will never see anything like it ever again.

Cook kept Yook Jieh and me very busy for the first little while. We chopped vegetables, shredded the dried scallops he had soaking, and also shark's fin, until our fingers ached. He was kind and did not yell at us — not like Mrs. Mah, who kept poking into the kitchen and telling us to work, not chitchat. Cook even stood up for us and told Mrs. Mah that we could do both, and that he liked to hear our voices and giggles, as it reminded him of his daughters in Hong Kong. Mrs. Mah sniffed and wrinkled her mouth like she was eating salted plums. Whenever she left the kitchen, Cook sneaked us a taste of each dish. It was rich man's food, like no food I've ever had before. Yook Jieh is lucky to live in the Mahs' household, even if she is only a *muui-jaai*. The shark's fin soup was my favourite — I did not know that shark's fin is pulled apart into shreds that look like shiny wires. They glisten in the soup, making your lips sticky with their richness.

I lost count of all the courses, there were so many. When we weren't helping with the food, we washed dishes. Mrs. Mah kept inspecting them, but she found none that were still dirty. It made me feel uncomfortable and I thought that maybe Yook Jieh was not so lucky after all, and told her so. She laughed. I like it when she laughs. Her eyes scrunch up and her face gets round. She told me that Mrs. Mah is just nervous, worried about the important people they are entertaining tonight. As mistresses go, Mrs. Mah is kind, she has only beaten Yook Jieh once, and that was because she ruined Mrs. Mah's best dress. My life seems hard to me, but I would not like to be a *muui-jaai*. I understand why Yook Jieh's family sold her to Mrs. Mah, but I am glad that such a thing did not happen to me!

When the meal was done, Mrs. Mah said we could come and listen to the speech her husband was going to make, as long as we stayed out of sight in the corridor. Cook made a funny noise and said he'd heard enough speeches like that to last his whole life, and that nothing ever came of them. He sat down and started eating. I could tell by Mrs. Mah's stiff back that Cook had dented her pride. My listening to the speech meant little to her; she had no need to impress me.

I was happy to listen to a speech, however long it was, if it gave me a chance to see the whole house. I've only ever seen the kitchen and Yook Jieh's room just off it. I had not realized how big the house was; it looks small from the street. Yook Jieh led me through corridor after corridor, all with rooms off them. The corridors ran the length of the house, and the room on the third floor, where the banquet was held, covered one whole side of the house. I just stared. You could probably fit seven of our rooms into it. The room was beautiful, with walls of wood that reflected the candlelight. At one end were two portraits, of a man and a woman. Yook Jieh whispered that they were the Mahs' ancestors. The room was full of men in western suits. They were sitting with their chairs pushed back so they could see Mr. Mah at the end of the table. Baba used to have a suit like that; we had a picture he sent to Ma and me. Now all he wears is his blue houseboy tunic and pants. I wonder what happened to that suit?

Cook was right not to come; the speech was very long. Mr. Mah's voice is thin, but he spoke passionately about China, about how Sun Yat-sen is the only man who can bring order and defeat the warlords. I have the same birthday as the great Dr. Sun Yat-sen, and Baba teases me that maybe I am destined to do great things too. Mr. Mah's speech worried me — all that talk of warlords and fighting. What must it be like for Ma? This is why it is so important for her to come here.

When Mr. Mah finished everyone clapped and then a servant carried around a chest, a beautiful chest with a metal clasp. The men stuffed money into it: money for Sun Yat-sen's army. Notes were sticking out of the chest by the time they had finished. I tried to imagine how much money that could be, but my mind wasn't big enough.

I was happy that at the end of the night Cook gave me a parcel of food to take away, enough for me, Baba and Mr. Chee. We will have a feast this afternoon.

Mrs. Mah gave me fifty cents. I will give it to Baba when he comes home from his morning at the Baldwins', to add to our savings.

As I write, I am looking out of the window. The tall white lady is here again, going into a building alongside the church. I wonder who she is.

### Monday, November 20

I got to the Lees' bright and early, so as to make Mrs. Lee impressed. It is easy for me to do that because I always wake when Baba rises and make him tea before he leaves. I had thought it would be like playing to look after the children, but it was not. They are like little jumping frogs, always on the move. Only the baby is still, but he makes up for that with noise.

The children were all up when I got there, but not dressed. That is to be my job while Mrs. Lee prepares breakfast. Her husband was already in the store and let me in, telling me just to go up the stairs behind the back room. He has a scowling face and seemed annoyed to be disturbed by me. All four children sleep in one room with their beds along the walls. In the centre of the room there is a table and this is where they take their meals. So I had to dress them quickly and then make the beds too. I did not know children wriggled so much. If it hadn't been for Lily, I would not have been able to do it. She showed me where their clothes were — stowed in baskets under their beds — and where they should wash. The Lees have a bathroom all their own! They don't have to collect water in a pitcher, like we do for the basin in our room.

Lily is funny. She is little, like a doll, but she is fierce with her brothers and sister, especially Arthur. He is the next oldest one and very wild. Mrs. Lee said I must use the children's English names as it is their father's wish; he wants them to be only Canadian. So it is Lily, Arthur, Rose and Hubert. The new baby will be Charles if it is a boy, and Agnes if it is a girl.

For breakfast Mrs. Lee made *jook* with dried shredded pork sprinkled on top. I fed Hubert his. It smelled very good and I was glad that I had eaten some cold rice with my tea before I came, because Mrs. Lee did not offer me any. It was not easy feeding Hubert. He kept grabbing the spoon and I was worried that the sticky rice porridge would go all over me. I had thought that babies were sweet and cuddly. What if my brother is like Hubert, crying all the time and difficult? No, he is older. He is three. By the time he comes, he will be four, Arthur's age. *Ai-yah!* That is worse to think about. He could be wild and spoiled because he is the only boy in the family.

I was glad when school time came because my ears hurt from all the noise the Lees made. I think Mrs. Lee was pleased because she said I had been a help.

Lily was sweet walking to school. She held my hand and told me about her friends. The mention of friends made me worry. I don't have many friends, only Bess, and what if some of the others teased me, like Ivor? I had Lily to protect now. I made her walk fast but no one bothered us.

Bess was waiting for me once I dropped Lily off with her friends. She was very glum. The good thing was that Ivor was not at school today.

美

I did not feel so strange at the Lees' today. I just have to be more careful when feeding Hubert. My bad dream came true and he batted a big spoonful of *jook* all over the front of my blouse. I gasped out loud. Mrs. Lee washed it off for me with a cloth, but it left my blouse very wet, and I could still see a whitey stain on the blue. Mrs. Lee said that I should set off for school early with Lily and then stop to change my clothes. I did not want to do this at all, but she insisted, so I had no choice. When we got into the street and I started walking to school, Lily was very puzzled. I told her that my blouse was almost dry and that it would be by the time we got to school. She whined that she wanted to see where I lived with my Baba. I felt ashamed and angry. I could not say to her that I had only one other blouse and that it was wet because I had washed it this morning, so it would be clean for school tomorrow. Lily would not understand; she has many clothes, some her mother sews for her, and even some that come from stores.

Lily stamped her foot and for a moment she looked just like her brother. She would not move until I promised that she could come and see our restaurant one afternoon after school. I do not know if that was the right thing to do. Should I just take her or should I ask her mother first?

While we were standing there I saw the tall white woman again. She is here very often, both early and late. She saw me too, because she smiled and waved.

Something is wrong with Bess, but she will not say what. She is not her smiling self and she is very quiet. Even Mr. Hughes noticed and asked her if she was sick. He is always telling Bess off for chattering — not to me, because she knows I will not whisper in class — but to Ada and Maisie in front.

Baba has written a letter to Ma. He writes beautifully, each character perfectly formed. Uncle Wing-lok was a scribe and taught him when Baba first came here as a boy. He will find someone going home to visit his family, and send the letter and some money with them.

I hope that Ma buys good medicine and that it will help Grandmother. When I was a little girl, Grandmother used to tell me stories about the monkey king. She had clever fingers and would pinch little characters out of mud to act the stories for me. I can remember what they looked like, but sometimes it is hard to remember Grandmother's face.

## Wednesday, November 22

It rained this morning — just a little, but my shoes were very soggy. They take a long time to dry and my feet get very cold. They also smell bad — but I am lucky, no one seems to notice.

It was a long day at school today: thoughts of Ma and Grandmother made it drag very much, and Bess was away so I had no one to talk to. I looked for Declan to ask where Bess was, but he ran off when I got near him and, later, he was always with Ivor.

I tried so hard to concentrate. Bess's empty seat made me feel lonely and I kept looking at it, remembering my first day at school. I was very frightened that day, because I had never ever been to a school before. Bess was the person who took my fear away. She was the only one in the room with an empty seat next to her, so the teacher sent me there. Bess started whispering to me at once, until the teacher scolded her. I was shocked and scared, thinking I was in trouble too, but Bess did not hang her head. I sneaked glances at this brave girl. She was strange looking to me then, Diary, with wild blond hair that looked like a nest of curly snakes. When she saw me looking, she winked and smiled.

On that long ago day, when recess came Bess grabbed my arm and made me walk with her. She did not mind that my English was poor. She told the others that I was going to be her friend. I remember how some of them laughed — not kind laughter, but mean, to match their faces — and said things to Bess that I didn't understand then. Now I can guess what they were saying, the same things they say now, the things that hurt Bess, but which she pretends mean nothing to her. They mock her clothes, laugh at her family and tell her she's dirty. I don't care! My clothes may be cleaner than Bess's, but they are not good either. Bess has a strong and kind heart.

I hope that she is all right and that she will be back soon.

Ah, Diary, so many people to worry about.

### Thursday, November 23

It is still wet and miserable. My shoes never seem to be dry these days. I have taken them and my stockings off while I write. My feet are all blotchy and red and stinging.

I have spent the day feeling sorry for myself, Diary, and that is not good. Bess is still absent. I caught Declan by himself, but he stuck his tongue out rudely and told me to mind my own business. Even though Lily is sweet-natured, being with her did not cheer me up much. It took something very surprising to do that.

I was walking to our restaurant when I heard a shout behind me. I kept my eyes down like Baba tells me to do — the men who hang around the street always catcall at people passing by, especially a girl like me who is sometimes alone. Baba says the men are disrespectful. He gets angry because he is unable to be with me and shield me from their remarks. The men have nicknames for all the girls they see. Some of them are very rude, Diary, and I will not write them down in your pages. What they call me is not rude to me, but it is to Baba — they call me Big Loser's Daughter. It makes me sad every time they yell it. Baba may have lost much, but he works so hard to make things right.

This is hard, Diary. It is so easy to go astray, because writing in you is like talking to a friend. Should I cross out all about the men? No, I will go back to the shout, the unusual shout. It was a woman shouting. She was speaking English, and she knew my name. "Wait!" is what I heard. "Wait, May Chin!"

It was the tall blond lady I have seen before and she was hurrying toward me. I didn't know what to do. I felt very shy and puzzled because she knew who *I* was, when I did not know her.

Even before she got to me she started talking and I found her hard to understand. Her voice is different from my teacher's. She talks fast and the words sound like they are being stamped out. Her name is Miss MacDonald and she is working at the church. She is a friend of my teacher and it is he who told her about me. Why, I do not know, because I am just a very ordinary girl. Even more strange, she wants me to go to tea with her on Saturday.

I have never been invited to tea. It is very exciting. I hope Baba says yes.

### Friday, November 24

Today is a good day, even though Bess is still away.

Mrs. Lee paid me my first wages. She seemed happy with the way I worked. Her husband looked grumpy, just like he always does. I was very proud to give the money to Baba. He smiled and praised me for my hard work. This also made me very proud.

I did not know what to do first, give Baba the money or ask him about having tea with Miss MacDonald. (What a funny name that is — it sounds like a cough!) I wanted to ask him yesterday, but he was very late. Mrs. Baldwin made him stay and do all the laundry all over again. One of the boys had left a pen in his pocket and the ink went everywhere. When he got to the restaurant, Baba's face was pale, and I could see that he struggled to help Wong Bak, so I waited, even though it was hard. All day I kept worrying about what he would say.

Today he was much more cheerful. He listened carefully to me, his head on one side the way it always is when he is thinking. At first he didn't say anything, and I felt very glum, sure that he would refuse.

Then the questions started, so many questions, but one over and over, "Why is this woman interested in you?" All I could tell him was that she was a friend of my teacher who had spoken of me to her.

Baba sighed and stopped slicing beef. His face

was sad as he told me how much he worried for me here, left alone so much, surrounded by so many rough men.

I felt tears then, Diary, but did not want them to fall. I know, even though no one has said it directly to me, that when Baba returned to China it was not to bring *me* back with him, but to bring my Ma. It was my grandfather who changed his mind. He told Baba — and this makes me go red writing it — that I was a clever girl, clever like Baba was, and that I needed to be schooled, something that would not happen if I stayed in China. Grandfather joked and said that Baba should remember my lucky birthday. Baba argued, but Grandfather would not change his mind, not even when Baba said that I would work the land with them more now that I was older. Grandfather said that they would manage, and if they needed, with the money that Baba sends they could hire a man to labour on our fields. I often worry that Baba regrets that he listened to Grandfather, especially when he came back to find Uncle Wing-lok dead, and all his money gone.

I told Baba that he was not to worry about me — that Mr. Chee, Wong Bak and Tsung Sook all look after me when he cannot be there. That I was a fortunate girl to be here in Gold Mountain with so many kind "uncles."

Baba smiled and made me happy when he said I was a dutiful daughter, always making the best of things. "Go to your tea," he said. "What harm can it do? Perhaps you may need a foreign friend, Ah-Mei."

I am very happy, so happy I could hop like a rabbit.

### Saturday, November 25

Oh, Diary, my chores seemed never ending today. I felt silly that this tea was so important to me. Yet that did not stop me boasting about it to Yook Jieh when I saw her in front of the Mahs' house. She was sad that I cannot visit her this afternoon, as she has something to tell me.

I made myself as tidy as I could, brushing my hair until it shone. I put my clean blouse under my mattress last night so that it would have no creases.

Mr. Chee walked me over to the building by the church, grumbling a little. He does not approve of the church and what he calls the *gwei lo* who work there. I do not think it is polite to call them foreign devils like this. This is their country and to them we are the foreigners! He waited until he saw the door open and then shuffled quickly off as if he did not want to be seen. He will stay in Mr. Lee's store and I know he will be watching until I leave, and then we will walk to the restaurant together.

Miss MacDonald is very tall. She is taller than Baba! Her nose is sharp like the beak of a bird. She reminds me of a heron! Am I being rude? I don't mean to be, but she is very funny looking.

Tea was in a room called the parlour. I would like to have a parlour. It was a beautiful room. The walls had paper with pink roses on it, and there were chairs with padded seats that matched. When you sat on them, they sank down. A little round table was set with tea things. My favourite was a plate like a tower in three parts around a pole. On the bottom part was what Miss MacDonald said was bread and butter. I liked the bread, but not the butter — that tasted bad, like milk that had soured. The next plate had buns, sticky with currants, which I liked. The top plate was the prettiest: little square cakes covered in pale, pale-coloured stuff, pink, yellow and blue. Each cake had little white sugar flowers on top. Miss MacDonald must have noticed me looking at them because she told me they were called iced fancies. I liked that name, but only the name was good, as the cakes were dry inside and the icing was very sweet.

I sound like a greedy girl, talking about nothing but the food, Diary, but it was all so very new. While I ate, Miss MacDonald asked me so many questions: questions about my Baba, and my Ma. I told her that we were saving hard to pay the government tax and that maybe this time next year, Ma and Little Brother would be here with us. She shook her head, and I thought she was saying it couldn't be done, so I told her how Baba worked as a houseboy, and about the restaurant, even about my job with the Lees. She told me that she didn't doubt that we were hardworking, she was just sad that we should have to pay this tax, and that it would be so much better in Chinatown if the men could bring their families here. My mouth fell open. I thought all Canadians did not want us here.

I wanted to hear more, to find out why she wanted to talk to me, but there was a big bonging noise, four times it came, and I saw it was a clock. I stood up fast and told her I must go because on Saturdays our restaurant is so busy, sometimes even with Canadian customers, and that Wong Bak and Tsung Sook need me there to take their orders, even though it is not really proper for me to do so. Miss MacDonald sighed and said that I must come again. I would like that.

### Sunday, November 26

It has been a quiet day, but a good one. I have thought a lot about Miss MacDonald. She is nice but strange. Maybe she has a job for me. Then I can earn more money.

Baba and I spent the afternoon quietly together in our room. Baba read a newspaper, and I read a little too; but a lot of the time, I watched Baba. Sometimes it seems like my eyes cannot see him enough. Perhaps because until I was eight and he returned home, he was just a man in a photograph and in stories that Ma told me — a hardworking, clever boy who was chosen by his uncle to go to Gold Mountain with him. His return was a big event in our village. I remember going from door to door with Baba as he gave a gift of strange, foreign food in cans to each household. *Ai-yah*, it was a fine time!

On the journey here Baba promised we would have many such fine times in Canada. He told me how I would be a respected merchant's daughter now that he and Uncle Wing-lok had set up a trading company with two others. Oh, Diary, I still see Baba's face when Wing-lok was not there to greet us. It was white with sorrow when he learned of Uncle's death and that the partners claimed there was no money for Baba, because it had been used to pay Wing-lok's gambling debts. He scared me when he shouted that Wing-lok was no gambler. Only Wong Bak, Uncle's friend from the old days, could calm Baba down. Without him, I do not know what would have happened to us. He found us our room, Baba's job, and then suggested the restaurant. It is through him that our fortune is turning. We are lucky to have such a friend!

### Monday, November 27

Such gloomy thoughts yesterday. Today I decided I would work at being more cheerful, and it was not hard because good things happened.

The Lee children are getting easier for me, now that they know me. Arthur is the annoying one, but Lily helps with him, although I dread when he starts school and will walk with us!

The best thing of all was that Bess is back! She would not say why she had been away, even though I did ask her. She does not look well: her skin is yellowish like her hair. I am puzzled. If she has been ill, why would she not tell me?

I had so much to tell her, and for once I could because she seemed tired and did not interrupt me like she usually does. In fact, our only interruption was Ivor Jones, who came up and asked Bess a question. He wanted to know whether everything was all right at home, but he laughed when he said it, and she did not answer him. I thought Bess looked like she might cry, but she rubbed her eyes hard and asked me about Miss MacDonald. Bess thought the tea sounded grand and very fancy. She said something strange though: "Watch out, Mei-ling, she's probably trying to convert you!" Then she called Miss MacDonald a do-gooder, which sounds like a nice thing to be, but Bess's voice made it seem bad.

Only one bad thing today, so much rain — my poor chilled, wet feet!

### Thursday, November 30

Two days with no writing here. Diary, you must think I have forgotten all about you, but that is not the case. I have had nothing to write about, truly. Each day is the same: go to the Lees', go to school, help Wong Bak in the restaurant, do my homework, walk home with Baba, go to bed.

So what is different today?

I saw Miss MacDonald. She was waiting for me outside our lodging house after I had taken Lily home. I think she wanted me to invite her to our room, but I could not. I would have been embarrassed for her to see how small it is, especially when she is used to such fine rooms. She asked if I would come to the church with her, but I did not want to do that. I have never been in a church. Baba does not speak out against church, like some, but we do not go. Also, Wong Bak was expecting me, so she walked with me, talking as we went.

I am almost embarrassed to write what Miss MacDonald said, Diary, because I will sound like a swollen-headed girl. She is interested in me because there are so few girls my age in Chinatown, and she wondered what the story of my life was. She has seen me coming from school, so asked Mr. Hughes, whom she knew from church, and he told her my name. She said that he told her that I was one of the cleverest students he has ever had. That made my cheeks get very hot, and I could not look at her. He also told her that he thought I could go on to high school, but perhaps would need some extra help. She laughed then, and said that is where she came in. I thought this was silly because she was already here. At her church, they run English classes for some of the younger men, and boys still in school. Some boys even sleep in a big room there. Miss MacDonald thinks maybe I could study at the church too.

I wanted her to go then, because this was foolishness; it could not be. "I cannot go to high school," I told her, "I must work more!"

She stopped walking and took my hands in hers, so that I had to stop too. "Think about it, May," she begged me. "High school is almost two years away; a lot could happen by then."

Miss MacDonald wanted to know if it was the boys that bothered me. I did not say anything. She said that I would work just with her, for maybe an hour each day. "Oh, do say yes, May! Maybe if other girls saw you studying with us, they might come too."

That made me think. Yook Jieh does not speak any English and I know she would like to learn. It also made me feel like a bad friend, because I still have not been to see her.

We were at the restaurant, and Wong Bak was sitting on a crate in front, smoking a pipe. He stood up as we approached. It made me realize how small he is, how hunched over he has become, as Miss MacDonald was so much taller. Miss MacDonald stepped toward him with her hand outstretched. He grinned and shook it, but said nothing, indicating with his head that I should go inside with him.

"Think about it, May!" Those words followed me in and lodged in my head. It is such a flattering, tempting offer. Maybe we would work in that beautiful parlour!

### Friday, December 1

Yesterday Wong Bak told Baba about Miss MacDonald almost before Baba was through the restaurant door. Baba looked stern and wanted to know if this lady was bothering me. I told him all she said. The only time he smiled was when I told him my teacher's words about me. He told me that I took after him, that he too would have been a scholar if he had been given the chance. My hopes rose just a little. I know it is selfish of me, Diary, and I said I would leave school as soon as I could, but I do love to study. Maybe if

I studied more, I could have a really good job and earn lots and lots of money!

Baba did not give me an answer then. He said he wanted to think about it some more. All that evening I caught him looking at me when he thought I would not notice. He, Wong Bak and Tsung Sook kept having whispered conversations. I tried to hear but only caught Tsung Sook saying that he wished he had had such an opportunity when he was my age.

This morning before he left for work, Baba told me that I can do extra study with Miss Mac-Donald, but only on condition that I get to the restaurant by five and work extra hard. I am lucky to have such a modern-thinking Baba! Now I just hope that this will suit Miss Mac-Donald.

I had great luck at school today too. Bess was more cheerful and has invited me on an adventure. Tomorrow, in the morning, there is a big event at Woodward's. Bess wouldn't say what it was, just laughed and said I would enjoy it. I know I should have asked Baba's permission, but I have asked for so many things lately. It is just a little way away, and I will be with Bess. I will be back before anyone knows I am gone!

I wish I had never gone! This has been a terrible day. I don't even want to write about it, Diary, but if I do, perhaps it will help me make sense of what happened.

Bess was waiting for me on the corner of Hastings and Carrall Streets, Declan with her. He did not look happy and neither did she. Mr. Chee had walked with me, grumbling all the time about how I always run after foreign devils. When he saw Bess and Declan he spat noisily on the street before turning away.

Woodward's is a huge building, and it was like a boat surrounded by a sea of people, all looking up at its roof. I wanted to go straight inside, but Bess pulled me back and told me to wait, as we were going to see Father Christmas arrive on the roof. She said something then that I did not understand, but which now makes a very horrible sense. She said she didn't want to go into the store until it was very, very full of people.

I had thought Father Christmas was just a story — but he is not! I saw him on the roof and he went down a chimney. Bess sniffed and said that this was something for stupid little kids. I wanted to watch and listen, but I felt shy because I was a big girl, and the only Chinese face there. I kept expecting someone to send me away.

It was then the day was spoiled. Bess pulled me into the store and dragged me along with her until we were behind a crowd of people. There was a pile of little dolls on a table. Bess called them kewpies. She told me to stand in front of her, so that people could not see her. Then, moving quickly like a snake striking, she pushed some of the dolls up inside the sleeves of her coat.

Words choked in my throat. I tried to say her name, tell her that she must not do this, but nothing came out.

"Don't stand there, gawping, Mei-ling!" Bess hissed at me. "Let's get out of here."

I wanted that very much, in fact I wanted to run as fast as my feet could carry me. What if someone had seen Bess? What if they thought I, too, had taken things? Would I be sent back to China? What shame this would be for my family. All our dreams would be broken like pot shards.

Bess did not let me run. She put her arm though mine, like she does in the yard at recess. "Walk slowly, don't act guilty," she warned me.

We *are* guilty, I wanted to tell her, but I had no words for her.

When we reached the sidewalk I pulled free and ran. I ran as fast as I could. I would not listen to Bess shouting after me. I did not feel my feet splash through the puddles. I ran and ran until I was safe here in our room with you, Diary. I

Someone is knocking on our door. It must be Mr. Chee — time to go to the restaurant. How can I face Baba and the others? They will surely know.

### Sunday, December 3

I do not know how I got through last night. Mr. Chee told on me. He told Baba, Wong Bak, Tsung Sook and anyone who would listen how I wanted to be with the foreign devils. Baba did not shout at me, but his face was sad that I had gone without telling him. He told me again that the one thing that worries him most of all is how badly people might treat me because I am a Chinese girl. Now it was like I was seeking out an opportunity to be hurt by going to big Canadian places. I wailed inside my heart to have given him such sadness — but that is not all. If he knew what my friend had done, and how I had been there, there would have been great anger too. My voice could only say little, that I was very sorry and would not go out with Bess again. That was easy, Diary, I do not want to go on her "adventures" ever, ever again.

I am very, very tired. I could not sleep last night. I kept thinking of what Bess did. Why would she take those things? It was not a quick thing that came to her when she saw the dolls; she had planned it. Did she think that I would help her or want to take things too? Was Declan somewhere else in the store, also taking things? What will I say to her tomorrow?

Another thing saddens me, Diary. I have been a selfish girl in so many ways lately. Oh, I have thought myself good because I have earned money, but I have thought only of things happening to me. I have not been thinking about Ma. The money for medicine will not reach her quickly. Will she be able to borrow money to pay for it? How is Grandmother? It is hard because they are so far away; it is easy just to think of here. Even here, I have not been a good friend. I have ignored Mr. Chee and Yook Jieh.

美

My feet dragged to school today. Lily's chatter did not make the worms inside my stomach stop twisting. In fact, it made them worse. She talked about nothing but the Father Christmas at Woodward's — her father had taken her and Arthur there to see him. She has asked him for a doll that says "Mama." My heart jumped even more when she said she had seen me there, until I realized that she had only seen me outside.

Bess was waiting for me as usual. Before I could speak, she linked her arm through mine, asking why I had run off on Saturday. My mouth fell open and I tried to say about what had happened, but she started talking over me, her voice loud and very cheerful. "Didn't we have fun?" she asked me. Then she started laughing about how fat Father Christmas was, and how shocked I had looked when he squeezed down the chimney. I felt like I was a crazy girl who perhaps imagined things. How could Bess act like nothing had happened? Every time I tried to talk about Saturday, she would talk over me in that strange voice, the one that tried to sound jolly, speaking about things that did not matter, like the colour of Ada Howe's dress or the way Mr.

Hughes wags his head when he is being serious. Bess's eyes were not jolly, though. The look in them stopped me from being mad with her. I stopped trying to talk about Saturday. I am very confused and wish I could forget it. This is what Bess wants, I think. Why did she steal the dolls? Why is she being like this?

To add to my unhappiness, it has become very, very cold. My feet hurt all the time — they ache and burn. Tomorrow I will try putting paper inside my shoes to keep the cold out and make the soles thicker.

The only good thing today was that I saw Miss MacDonald and told her that my Baba had said I may come to her for help with school-work, but only for the little while between the end of school and when I go to the restaurant. She clapped her hands, saying, "Oh, May, that is capital!" I did not understand what it was she said, but her smile told me that she was happy. We have agreed that we will start next week, and I am to tell Mr. Hughes so that he may set extra work for us. I should feel very happy and lucky, but it is made sour by my worry over Bess.

美

I feel like I have turned into an ice girl. I cannot get warm. I wore both my blouses today, one on top of the other. It only helped a little. As I write in you, Diary, I am wrapped in a blanket, with only my hands and face showing. The paper in my shoes is useless. All it did was crinkle and make a noise. It also caused me much trouble.

Ivor saw the paper poking out and laughed. "Is that what you wear in Chinky China?" he asked. "Or don't you wear shoes at all?"

Bess told him to shut up. He turned on her then, laughing about how she had no stockings. He was very mean and pushed her over. One of her shoes came off and he grabbed it and ran around the schoolyard, waving it and yelling at people that Bess Murphy's shoes had more hole than sole. Nearly everyone laughed. I was surprised because Bess just sat on the ground, her head bent so that her hair hid her face. I had expected her to get up and punch him — that is what she normally would do.

Ivor danced in front of Bess, dangling her shoe, and singing "Bog Irish! Bog Irish!" I do not know what this means, but I knew it was meant to hurt like a stone thrown at Bess. Others circled round and started the hurtful yelling too.

Still Bess did not do anything. I could not see her face, but I heard her sob. It made my heart ache so much that I surprised myself. I ran at Ivor, snatched the shoe from him and yelled at him to leave her alone. For just a tiny bit, he was so shocked that he did nothing. Then he started to move toward me, his fist raised.

I was very lucky because Mr. Hughes came then. He wanted to know what was happening. The crowd disappeared very quickly. Ivor started to say it was a game we were playing.

"It was not!" The words fell out of my mouth before I could stop them. "Ivor was teasing Bess. He made her cry." I put my hand over my mouth to silence myself, but it was too late. Mr. Hughes grabbed Ivor by the arm, dragging him toward the school. He was talking all the time, shouting really, about how he was tired of Ivor's mean tricks. I knelt down to give Bess her shoe. As I did I saw Ivor turn his head and mouth something at me. I think he said, "Just you wait, May Chin!"

I am glad I helped Bess. She has always stood up for me, but now I am a little scared.

Nothing happened today. That is a silly thing to write, but I mean that Ivor did nothing to me, except give me mean looks. Mr. Hughes thrashed him yesterday. He also scolded the whole class and told us he is made sick by the way we taunt each other about where we come from. It is mainly the boys. They make gangs and fight: Japanese against Portuguese, Italians against Japanese, Portuguese against Italians, English against . . . I could go on and on, Diary. There are not enough Chinese boys to form a gang, so we just get picked on by everyone. At first I could not see why Mr. Hughes was saying this to us, but then I remembered what Ivor had called Bess. Ivor is always quick to make fun of people's families and customs. He is very proud of the fact that he is British. Mr. Hughes said we should celebrate that we are all Canadians now. Looking straight at Ivor and at John Kobayashi, he said that he would punish anyone he caught fighting like this or calling names. He can be very fierce. I hope that Ivor will remember this fierceness.

I liked what Mr. Hughes said about being Canadian, but now it is making me sad. Twenty-four years my Baba has lived and worked in Canada, longer than he was in China, but I don't think people see him as Canadian, do they? If they did, he could have his family here so easily and we would all be happy.

Ah, I must not write gloomy thoughts. If I look out of my window, it is beautiful. We had snow! Just a little, but it makes everything look clean.

Yook Jieh is standing in the doorway of the Mahs' house. She has seen me and is waving.

### Thursday, December 7

I am still an ice girl. Everyone is shaking their heads about how cold the weather has been. I am glad at school for the stove, and glad that Bess and I sit near it. I worry about Baba and his journey to work. His coat is very thin and he has no gloves. At least the Baldwins' house is warm and he tells me that the kitchen is hot, once he starts the day's cooking. Yesterday Mrs. Baldwin asked him to shovel the snow from the pathways, and even though he did not complain to me, I think he was very cold. Perhaps I can make him some mittens as a gift for the Winter Solstice Festival.

Ivor was not in school today. Declan says he has a cold. A mean part of me was glad. I have given up trying to talk to Bess about what she did. She will not listen, and when I tried very hard to make her, she asked Mr. Hughes if she could change seats and sit with Ada. My heart got all empty, but I was lucky that Mr. Hughes said she could not change her seat for a whim.

Oh, Diary, I am writing the little details, when I have big news.

Yook Jieh was still waiting for me when Mr. Chee and I set off for the restaurant yesterday. He grumbled when I stopped to talk to her, but the Mahs' cook invited him to sit in the kitchen and have some tea. I think Cook fed him a little too, because Mr. Chee seemed very happy when we set out again.

The big news is not my news, but Yook Jieh's. Some of the bachelors have started coming around to see Mr. Mah, wanting to marry her, and he has said that he will find a suitable match! She giggled and her face got very pink when she told me how she hid behind the kitchen door and listened to Mr. Mah greet some of them. Four different men have visited. They bring him gifts. One even brought a bottle of whisky.

Yook Jieh to be married, *Ai-yah!* She seemed so happy that I felt mean when some words flew out of my mouth: "Will you choose or will Mr. Mah?" Even as I spoke I knew the answer, and it made me sad. Yook Jieh is Mr. Mah's *muui-jaai* and he will take whatever is offered as a bride price; that is the way it works.

She just laughed, telling me that Mrs. Mah has promised that they will choose a young, handsome husband for her. I did not say anything more. Young, handsome men do not have money — our friend Tsung Sook is just such a one.

### Friday, December 8

I was going to write more about Yook Jieh, but we have much snow. It fills my head and not just the streets.

It was difficult to walk. Poor Lily struggled with it. Her feet kept slipping and she had to lift them high. When she started to cry I could not bear it, so I gave her a piggyback the last bit of our journey home. For such a little girl, she was heavy, but I managed. My teeth were clattering together, so I could hardly speak when I went into the Lees' store. Mrs. Lee was there and she cried out when she saw us. She made me come upstairs and have some hot tea while she changed Lily's wet clothes. Even the tea could not warm me, but it was nice to have some. It was the first time that Mrs. Lee has ever offered me food or drink. The Lees have a stove and the room was warm. I would have liked to stay there, but I also wanted to go home and change my stockings. My feet and legs were turned a funny blue colour, and they felt like hot needles were pricking them.

It has been a day of gifts for me, Diary. Mrs. Lee gave me twenty cents extra for taking such good care of Lily! They must be very rich to throw money so generously. I do not know whether this is a good thing to do, but I am not going to give that money to Baba. I shall buy wool and make him mittens. Is that very wrong of me? It is money we were not expecting. I knit well — Miss Clarke said so in Handicrafts.

The money was not Mrs. Lee's only gift to me. She brought a *min-naap* back with her from the bedroom and placed it around my shoulders. It was lovely. The padding inside the silk made it warm, and soon my teeth stopped banging. I went to hand it back to her when it was time to leave, but she waved it away and said that it was mine to keep. "It is old, Mei-ling, and does not fit me any more," she said. "See, how the silk is fraying on the jacket's cuffs?" I did not care. It was beautiful. I have never had so fine a garment before. It is like wearing a beautiful blue cloud. I am wearing it now as I write, and the ice girl has thawed.

I nearly forgot, I had one more gift — Ivor was still away!

## Saturday, December 9

It is quite late. The last customers are just leaving the restaurant and Baba and I will walk home soon. I worried about him yesterday, thinking Mrs. Baldwin would make him clear all that snow, but it was the gardener's day to come and he did it. Mrs. Baldwin has been kind to Baba too. She has given him some of Mr. Baldwin's old gloves. Baba sighed when he showed me them and shook his head. "What have we come to, Ah-Mei," he asked, "that we have to accept the kindness of others just to keep warm." I knew he was thinking about my *min-naap*. I feel very bad. I do not need the money I kept to buy wool for mittens now, and I should have given it straight to Baba, but how can I do that now without him thinking that I am a deceitful girl who hides things from him? Perhaps, next week, it can be a bonus.

It has not been a pleasant day, and I have had no time to write until now.

There was still more snow, not as much as yesterday, but maybe another two inches. Mr. Chee did not want to go this morning on our usual route. He does not look well. I took our washing to the laundry. It was no harder than usual, because I always carry it, but I forget how Mr. Chee acts as my guardian. Despite the snow, there were a lot of men on the streets, and they yelled to me. I do not look at them, but keep my eyes on the ground. "Talk to us, Big Loser's Daughter!" they shout or, "Don't be proud. Stop and pass the time of day and we will buy you *dim-sum*." That would be shameful, so I made my feet hurry. One man got up from the box where he was sitting and walked alongside me, talking all the time. "Pretty girl," he said, "do not ignore us. We mean you no harm. Let me carry your bag for you?" From the corner of my eye I saw his hand reach out and then I ran. I did not stop until I ran into someone, someone solid and tall who called out my name. It was Tsung Sook. He walked with me and then walked me home. The men turned their attention to him, making mean comments about how he was lucky to be such close friends with my father. He did not ignore them and taunted them back, calling them wastrels who sit and gamble their money away. One of them spat at our feet as we walked by.

My day was made sour because of this. I have been thinking a lot about Yook Jieh, wondering if more suitors visited the Mahs today. With so few women here, the Mahs will get a good bride price for her. I hope they choose well for her — not an old, old man, because she is only fifteen. Fifteen is a good age to marry; Ma was fifteen when she was chosen for Baba's bride. Some girls are younger when they marry, it is true, but I am only just twelve. Do those rude men not know that? They seem to know everything else. Why would they want me to talk to them?

### Monday, December 11

Yesterday — my apologies, Diary — I did not write in you. I meant to, but Baba and Wong Bak and Tsung Sook asked me to play *mah joong* with them when the restaurant closed. Mr. Chee is normally the fourth player, but has a cold so he stayed in his room. I am not a very good player, but I am lucky!

In the afternoon I spent some time with Yook Jieh and yes, more men did come to visit Mr. Mah, because word has got out that he is looking for a match. She is happy. She says that her fortune will be made here in Gold Mountain. I hope it will be true.

It has been colder than ever. When will it end? Mr. Hughes was telling us that this is unusual weather. I do not care, I just want it to go away. Ivor was back. Sickness has not made him a nicer person, but he is such a crafty boy. He pokes and whispers mean things only when he knows that he will not be caught. All day he kept whispering, "Watch out, May Chin, I haven't forgotten that you got me into trouble. I'm going to make your life miserable!" I made sure that I stayed with Bess.

At the end of the day Mr. Hughes gave me a package of books to take to Miss MacDonald for us to work on. He is a very kind man. When I said this to Bess, she snorted and said, "Oh, May, can't you see he's sweet on that do-gooder and wants to impress her." It does not matter to me. I am just thankful.

It was wonderful. Mr. Hughes had put a note inside the package that arithmetic is my weakest subject, so that is what we concentrated upon. Miss MacDonald made it seem easy and, finally, fractions made sense to me. It is hard because the other students learned much before I even came to Canada. She has set me some sums for tomorrow, so this will be a short entry. We were in the parlour. I will definitely have a parlour when I am a grown-up woman!

## *Tuesday, December 12*

One month I have been writing in you, Diary, and I hope that I have done it right. It is hard for so many reasons, and it is getting harder, but I like doing it because I can talk about everything in your pages, and that is something I cannot do so easily with people. What happens at school, I cannot talk about with people here, in China-town — they would not understand, or Ivor Jones's meanness to me would worry them, or make them think that school is a bad thing. But it is not. Learning new things, that is the best thing of all. That makes my mind soar like a bird. I can *write* that, but if I said it to Wong Bak or Yook Jieh, they would look at me like I was a truly crazy girl.

Baba understands, I think, but I see him so

little and it is rare we talk of serious things. His mind is eaten up with worry about how we will get Ma and Little Brother here. I worry too, but I do not say because it will make Baba's worry all the bigger. I don't write about them much here, because I think of them so often that if I wrote it here, that's all there would be. It is not something easy to talk about either, and not to people like Bess and Miss MacDonald. Bess is not interested in what she calls "Chinese malarkey." Miss MacDonald is interested, always she has questions, but they make me uncomfortable and my answers are short. Some sorrows are private.

### Wednesday, December 13

My entries are getting shorter. Yesterday Baba made me stop because he wanted to sleep, and said that I should too. But often that is the only time I have to write in you, Diary, when we return from the restaurant late at night! I used to write in the morning, but now I do the extra work Miss MacDonald sets me before I go to the Lees' to look after the children. (The baby has two new teeth — he is much sweeter in his temper now!) After school I rush back and go straight to see Miss MacDonald. My school homework I do in the restaurant between my chores. I am always terrified that it will be spoiled if something is spilled upon it. I try not to risk *your* beauty there!

Baba is watching me as I write. He pretends he is reading *The Chinese Times*, which someone left in the restaurant tonight, but I see him sneaking little peeks at me. I hope I can finish before he wants us to sleep. He coughs too. I wonder if it is his way of getting my attention so that perhaps I will stop.

My last entries have sounded complaining, but I do not mean them to. I think other people may have far worse things to face than I do, like Bess. She has become quiet again and will not tell me what is wrong. "Nothing!" she says, but she won't look at me. Declan's face was all bruised today. He came and stood with us rather than play with the bigger boys. I wonder if Ivor beat him.

### Friday, December 15

I missed another day. I knew it would happen. Sometimes I am very selfish and think only of myself. Poor Baba was not false coughing. He has caught Mr. Chee's cold and it has been very bad. Last night he was so pale and tired-looking that I knew he must sleep as soon as we got home. I worry about him working so hard, and wish that he could stay home and rest, but he said that there are many who would be happy to take his place with the Baldwins if he should fail to go. I am keeping my fingers crossed (is that not a strange expression, because if I did, I could not write!) that he will recover soon. Mr. Chee is much better. He is a little weak, and his cough continues, but he was waiting for me outside the church today after my time with Miss MacDonald, and walked to the restaurant with me. It was nice to have a peaceful walk again, with no catcalls.

A whole week of lessons with Miss MacDonald! I have learned so much. Arithmetic has been our main study, but we have also worked on English and dictations. She is very kind, even if she is very nosey. She always has tea for me. Today she stopped our study early. She complimented me on my progress, even in just a week. She told me how her church has helped other Chinese young people with their studies. She told me of one girl, a girl from Victoria, and they are helping pay for her to become a doctor!

This is very shocking to me — a doctor! I did not know that girls can be doctors. That would be such a fine thing to do. If I became a doctor I could help all those people in Chinatown who fear going to the Canadian hospitals with their white doctors and nurses. Miss MacDonald laughed at my surprised face. "Mr. Hughes was right, May. You are a very clever girl. With the right opportunity and help, you could do anything you wanted to do!" she said.

### *Saturday, December 16*

Last night was a tossy-turny night as I tried to sleep, but could not. Baba was coughing a lot. I got up and made him hot water with ginger root and that seemed to help. But it was not just the coughing. It was Miss MacDonald's words; they ran in my head like dogs chasing cats. I know she told me about that girl because she wanted to encourage me, but she is wrong, wrong, wrong! I cannot do anything I want. Not even when we finally have Ma and Little Brother here. Then I must still work to make the family secure. It is so hard. Miss MacDonald means well, but what does she know of what it is like to be me?

I kept those thoughts out of my mind, Diary. I will not let myself dream. Working helped. I cleaned our little room, and then I cleaned Mr. Chee's. He grumbled at me and said that I made him feel tired because I was always moving like a spinning top, but he was pleased, I know. He is much better, but he is very thin after his cold.

It seems like everyone is happy now. I visited with Yook Jieh this afternoon and she is fluttery like a bird with excitement. Mrs. Mah has told her that they will choose her husband soon, so that she can be married by the New Year celebrations. That would be very fine. She worried me because she told me that one of her suitors last week came all the way from Victoria. I hope he is not the chosen one. I do not want Yook Jieh to go so far away, but maybe that is a selfish thought.

Wong Bak and Tsung Sook are also happy. Business has been good. This makes me happy too, for it will add to our savings. They want to plan a banquet to celebrate the Winter Solstice Festival next week. I had forgotten about the festival. They were laughing and planning who we might invite. They each have friends among the bachelors. I know that they would include Mr. Chee, but he might be invited to the Lees' too. Who would I invite? I would invite Yook Jieh of course, and, though I know it cannot be, I would dearly love to invite Bess. She could not come. She has never come into Chinatown.

*Ai-yah!* I have done it again. I am thinking always about here. Winter Solstice Festival is the time for *families* to come together. It is now the fourth year we are a family that is broken apart by the ocean!

### Sunday, December 17

Just a short time to write. After Baba left for work, I slept in. I have never done that before. I was very tired and had slept so little because of Baba's cough. It is loud and sounds like a motor car engine trying to start. I swear it made the screen around his bed shake.

I did not wake up until he came home just after lunch. He is not well. I persuaded him to go to bed and stay there. He tried to say that he must go to the restaurant later, but I was very fierce and said that Wong Bak would understand. I wished that I could have gone to the Baldwins' in his place this morning.

Wong Bak is a good man, and he did understand, but it meant I had to work extra hard, helping with preparation, while Tsung Sook did the serving. I am tired now, and will stop writing. Baba was sleeping deeply when I came home with Mr. Chee. I am using a candle to write by so as not to disturb him. He has not coughed. This is good.

### Monday, December 18

Both Bess and Declan were absent from school today. I do hope they are all right.

I felt like a little mouse, scurrying from place to place, looking over my shoulder all the time, just waiting for Ivor to pounce on me. It makes me sad, but I realize that, apart from Bess, I have no other friends at school. I haven't needed them because she has always been there. Ada Howe sometimes talks to Bess, but I do not feel brave enough to presume that she would talk to me.

Mr. Hughes let me stay inside at recess. There were some textbooks that needed covering and I asked if I might do that.

Poor Lily did not know what to make of me today. I bundled her into her coat and then we ran all the way home. I tried to say it was a game, but she did not look happy. There was no sign of Ivor.

## *Tuesday, December 19*

Ivor caught me today, Diary, but he is such a clever boy that I can do nothing. I am very sad, but I can tell no one but you.

We were in class, writing an essay. Mr. Hughes was writing some Maths problems on the board. Ivor put up his hand and asked if he might get some more ink for the well on his desk. When he was given permission, he went to the front and picked up the big flask of ink with the spout. As he walked back down the aisle to his seat behind me, he was grinning. Just as he came near, he pretended to stumble forward as if he had tripped on something, and he swung the ink bottle so that ink flew out all over my desk, my essay and, worst of all, me — great splashes of ink all over my white middy blouse. I cried out and Mr. Hughes turned. Ivor quickly said, "Oh, no! Look what I have done. I'm sorry, sir, but I tripped." Ink had hit his desk too, but only a little.

I am ashamed, because I cried. I sat there and

cried. Mr. Hughes was kind. He sent me to one of the lady teachers. She found me an old blouse to wear and soaked mine, but not all the ink came out. It hangs on the back of a chair as I write and I see the marks still, pale blue shadows. Mr. Hughes made Ivor clear up the mess on the desks, but did not punish him. How could he — it was just an accident, wasn't it? He did not hear Ivor later when he whispered in my ear, "That's just the start, May Chin!"

I do not want to write any more.

## Wednesday, December 20

I was alone again today. Bess and Declan are still away. All day I was on edge, but Ivor did nothing more to me. Well, nothing except smirking, and once he sort of jumped toward me in the corridor. I screamed and he laughed. I wish I were braver.

Baba is feeling better, much better, and that makes my heart very glad. I am very lucky as I do not seem to have caught anything from either him or Mr. Chee. Baba noticed my blouse last night and wanted to know what had happened. I am ashamed of myself but I lied to him. I said that *I* had dropped the ink bottle. I do not want him to worry. Nor do I want him to think he has not made a wise decision by sending me to school. I know how lucky I am. I think he believed me because he just grunted and said no more.

I am having to become a very sneaky girl in lots of ways. Even though it made me a little late, I changed my blouse last night before I went to Miss MacDonald. I did not want her asking me questions. She is such a determined person that it is hard not to answer her. I could just see her going to the school and telling Mr. Hughes what had happened, and that would be a very, very bad thing. My life is already being made miserable because I got Ivor into trouble.

### Thursday, December 21

Oh, I have surprised myself. Not even two full weeks and I have come to depend on going to see Miss MacDonald. Today will be the last time that she can see me until January, as she is going home to Ontario to visit her family. Her brother is a minister in Toronto. He has many children, she told me, and one of her nieces is just my age. She smiled and said that this niece reminds her of me, as she loves to learn too.

When it was time for me to go, Miss Mac-Donald stood up and took a package from the bureau and shoved it toward me. "It's a Christmas gift, May," she said. "I picked up one for my niece too." She seemed embarrassed and would not look at me. "I know you probably don't celebrate Christmas, but isn't one of your festivals at this time? Can it be a gift for that?"

My heart was very full. I knew it was a book, by the feel of the package, and knew it couldn't be a diary because I have told Miss MacDonald about you. She looked so awkward and hopeful all at the same time, so I told her that yes we do give each other presents at Winter Solstice, but I did not tell her that it is usually just family and that new clothes are the gift. She asked me to open it, and it was beautiful. It is a book called *Anne of Green Gables* by a lady called L.M. Montgomery. Miss MacDonald said that when I read it, I will see that Anne and I are a little alike. I have never ever owned a book before. I shall treasure it as much as I do you, Diary.

It has been a good day today. Only one more day of school, and I will not have to worry about Ivor until January. He kept sneaking up behind me again, but I tried to make sure that I was always where there were crowds. Bess is still not back, nor is Declan. I worry for them, even though I don't really like Declan.

### Friday, December 22

Lots more rain today, but I am no longer the ice girl, just the wet one! We stayed in at recess so it was easy to avoid Ivor. Ada's desk mate, Maisie, was away so she asked Mr. Hughes if I could move and sit with her. This was surprising to me — surprising that she would ask, and surprising that he agreed. He was very jolly today; all the teachers were. We did not have normal lessons, but sang carols, drew pictures and played word games and quizzes. I knew a lot of the answers, but felt shy about putting my hand up. Ivor did very well and he got an extra piece of the candy that Mr. Hughes had brought in for us. I decided to keep mine and share it with either Yook Jieh or Mr. Chee. It was chocolate. Some people had brought Mr. Hughes little gifts. I did not, and that made me feel very bad because he has been so kind to me. Ada said that she didn't have money to buy gifts so she had made him one, a pen wipe out of felt. She had embroidered it so that it looked like a flower that she called a pansy. It was very lovely. I shall do that, and I won't wait until next Christmas either, because he might not be my teacher then. I shall make him and Miss MacDonald something during the holidays.

There was good news too, when I took Lily home. I had thought that Mrs. Lee would not need me now that school was done for a while, but her baby is due soon, and she has asked me to come for much of the day, starting next week, to help mind the children. She will pay me 25¢ a day! I will be rich — that is, if Baba says I may go.

It was a lovely day, but it would have been lovelier if Bess had returned. I asked Ada if she knew what was wrong, but she said she had not seen any of the Murphys around their neighbourhood all this week. Now my worry is getting bigger.

## Saturday, December 23

This will be a long entry, Diary, to make up for how I have been neglecting you, and because it has been a special day, both sweet and bitter. Sweet because we celebrated the Winter Solstice Festival with a banquet just like Wong Bak and Tsung Sook planned, but bitter because all day thoughts of Ma flooded into my heart. It is a family time, and although we gathered with the friends who have become our family here, it made the absence of our real families harder to bear. I cried a little when I thought of China, picturing our simple house and the fields around it. Ma, Grandfather and Grandmother (I see Grandmother healthy in my mind, because that's how I want her to be) eating their special meal. I can't see my little brother so easily because he was born after I left for Gum Shan with Baba, but I know that he will be strong and sturdy. He has a strong, good name too — Sing-wah, which means "Arise, China!" I made sure my tears fell only when no one was there to see them.

It was a day when I kept a promise. I asked Mrs. Lee if Lily could visit the restaurant today. She has wanted to for such a long time. I took her this morning. It was very funny because with me she chatters like a little monkey, but when she met Wong Bak and Tsung Sook her words dried up. They were very kind, and Tsung Sook carved her a rose from a radish. Her "*M'goi*" was very quiet, but Tsung Sook smiled to hear her thanks.

Oh, our banquet was fine. In the restaurant,

the usual smells of onions and garlic were there, but I could also smell black beans. They are Baba's favourites. He had asked Mrs. Baldwin if he could come home early if he worked the whole day tomorrow, and she agreed. Mr. Chee and I spent most of the day at the restaurant. I was right, he was invited to the Lees too, but he is crafty and has arranged to eat with them tomorrow! He sat and drank tea while I helped Wong Bak and Tsung Sook with the preparations. I was surprised by my Baba. He was later than I thought, and when he came he had a bag with him — a bag from Woodward's. In it were two most beautiful middy waists, just my size, one pale blue and one pink. Best of all, they have detachable collars, so if I am careful, I can just wash those collars and not the whole blouse. I started to say that we needed to save our money, but he stopped me and said, "You need to have proper clothes too, Ah-Mei." I have the best, most thoughtful Baba in the whole world.

We closed the restaurant early. Our guests arrived and what food there was! Not the fancy rich man's food like the Mahs had at their banquet, but like the food Ma cooked at home. My mouth is filling with water just thinking about it! Everyone enjoyed it, smacking their lips and praising Wong Bak. We made chicken cooked three ways: steamed and white with a tasty sauce of oil, scallions and ginger; a rich, rich soup with beads of fat on the surface; and then while we sat around the table, Wong Bak stir-fried the gizzard, heart and liver with vegetables. There was a pork butt roast, braised with ginger and sugar, a big steamed fish, stir-fried beef and vegetable, and then the *Toong Yuan*. That soup made us all silent, and I could see memories rise in people's eyes. The little sticky rice balls bobbed on the surface of the soup, white ones and then some stained pink for good fortune. *Toong Yuan*. Oh, those words hurt when I thought about how their meaning can change if you pronounce them just a little differently — rice-ball soup, or family reunion. In all our different ways then, that is what we thought about, what we wanted. Baba patted my hand. His voice raspy, he said, "We will do it, Ah-Mei, if we work hard, we will do it!"

### Sunday, December 24

Why is it that my life switches from good to bad so quickly?

It is my own fault. I should listen more. My

Baba told me not to venture out of Chinatown after he found out I went to Woodward's with Bess, but I twisted his words in my head. I promised him that I would not go out with Bess again, and I didn't — I went looking *for* her. I know that is deceit, but I just had to find out why she and Declan had both missed school. Last night I could not sleep, thinking about how she has been such a good friend to me, almost like a sister. And how sad she had been, how bruised Declan was. Winter Solstice kept turning my thoughts to how important family and friends are. Bess would probably have just snorted and said that I had indigestion from too much rich food.

This morning, soon after Baba left for work, I sneaked out, creeping like a mouse so I would not draw Mr. Chee's attention. It is not far to Bess's house, but I have never been there. I did not know what I would say, or even know that I would say anything when I got there. Maybe I would see Declan playing on Union Street, and then I could go home happy.

Now I do not know what to do. The Murphys have gone.

When I knocked on the door, and I really did knock only quietly, a man wearing just an undershirt and trousers threw it open and shouted at me for disturbing him so early. He seemed very angry. He was very hairy, like an animal. His voice made mine very small when I asked if he was Mr. Murphy. His face got all red then, and he yelled some more, fast and loud with the spit flying from his mouth. I did not understand all he said, but, oh, Diary, I am so sad for Bess. The man said her father had gone, "had done a bunk." He got angrier and angrier, shouting like it was my fault. Nasty words came out, "Feckless, bloody Irish, spending their money on drink. They haven't paid the last two months' rent!" I think he was the landlord, because he boasted — boasted that he had put them out on the street where they belonged. How could anyone take pleasure in making people miserable like that?

I asked very politely, because I did not want to make him even angrier, if he knew where they had gone. It was very strange. It was like he only then saw me. "What's it to you, you little Chink?" he said, pushing his face close to mine.

I shrank away, backing down the steps. I did not want to hear this man any more. He raised his arm like he would hit me. "Clear off out of here, you yellow heathen, disturbing decent people on Christmas Eve!"

I ran, oh how I ran, Diary. I did not look back until my own building was in my view. I did not even care about being quiet on the stairs. I slammed my door behind me and threw myself onto my bed.

It has taken me an hour to calm down. Writing what happened has helped, but oh, where are Bess and her family, what has become of them?

### Monday, January 1, 1923

Did you wonder what had happened to me, Diary? A whole week, and not one little word!

*Ai-yah*, it has been a time of scurrying and excitement. Mrs. Lee's baby was born soon after I finished writing last Sunday — another boy. Mr. Chee came hobbling over fast and said that I was needed there. I was scared, because I know nothing about helping a baby be born. It is so different here with no mother-in-law to help, or maybe a midwife. Mrs. Yip sometime acts as a midwife, but she was not there when Mr. Chee and I arrived. I could hear Mrs. Lee groaning and it made my heart stand still with fear. Lily had the children all sitting in the store, and that is where they stayed and Mr. Chee and I with them. That is what Mr. Lee wanted: Mr. Chee to mind the store, and me to watch over the children.

All day we were there. We sent a message to Wong Bak to say that we could not leave. It was very hard. I kept trying to think of games to keep the children busy, but the little ones' eyes were big and scared when they heard their mother. Singing songs, the songs my Ma used to sing me, worked best.

It was night before Mr. Lee came down and said that a boy had been born. He looked tired, but he smiled when he told us that it was a puny, ill-favoured baby. We smiled too, but Arthur did not understand. He started to cry and I had to explain that this meant just the opposite — the baby was strong and healthy, but it is ill luck to say so in case the ghosts and evil spirits become jealous. There was blood on Mr. Lee's apron, but thankfully the children did not notice.

All week I have been helping the Lees and I have not had a moment to myself, Diary, in which to write in you. I tried taking you there, but Arthur grabbed you when I started to write, so I did not do this again. You are too precious to be carelessly spoiled.

Mrs. Lee was very weak; she bled a lot. But she did not want to go to the hospital. That too would be ill luck, as she must stay inside for forty days after a baby's birth. So it was my job to care for the children and her. I am tired. Looking after children is hard work although they were good, even Arthur! I liked being there, being part of a family. Mrs. Lee talked more to me than she has ever done, telling me about her journey here when she was just sixteen. I had thought her very old, but now I realize she is younger than Ma, perhaps only twenty-four.

It was good to be busy. It gave me little time to think, but now as I sit and write the thoughts come back, the ones that bother me — thoughts about whether my grandmother is well again, whether our money reached her to buy good medicine. And then the here thoughts, because school starts tomorrow. I still have not made a gift for Mr. Hughes, but will try to do so soon. Has Ivor forgotten the threats he made? I doubt it, and without Bess how can I cope with such misery? Ah, that is a twisted thought because it thinks only of me, but what of Bess? Where is she?

美

## *Tuesday, January 2*

I am the happiest girl alive! Bess was in school! At first there was no sign of her, but she arrived, out of breath, just as Mr. Hughes was taking the register. She dropped down in the seat next to me like nothing had been wrong.

At recess we stayed inside because of the heavy rain, so I asked her.

"Declan and I were sick," she said. Her eyes were all flat and they would not look at me.

No, I thought to myself, this time I will not let her do this. So I told her how I had gone to her house and what the horrible landlord had said.

Tears ran down her face, but she made no noise, and now she looked at me. I put my arm around her shoulders. It was some time before she spoke. She said she didn't want people to know and that I wasn't to tell anyone else. I don't think you count, Diary, because no one reads you but me.

In November Bess's father lost his job on the docks. They dismissed him because he was unreliable through drink — those were her words. He did not go looking for another job, just hung around bars, hoping his friends would buy him drinks. Then he went away. They don't know where. Bess shocked me because she said that she hoped he'd gone to h——! Only Liam was earning some money, but it wasn't enough to keep the family, and it was hard for him because he was trying to save to get married. Do you remember, Diary, I told you how bruised Declan was and how I thought maybe it was Ivor who had done it? I feel very badly because it wasn't. It was Liam. Declan stole some coppers from their mother's purse, money that Liam had given her for food. This ended everything. Liam left too, and is lodging with the parents of the girl he wants to marry. When the landlord threw them out, Mrs. Murphy had no choice but to split the children up. She and the two little girls, the twins who are just four, they're staying with one aunt, and Bess and Declan with another.

"Oh, Bess," I said to her, "that is a terrible thing to happen."

She pulled away from me. When she spoke, her voice was sharp. "Don't you go feeling sorry for us, Mei-ling! I won't have it. We'll manage, just you see, I'll make sure of that!"

"By stealing?" Oh, Diary, as soon as those words came out, I wanted to eat them up again.

Bess was the old defiant Bess again. "Yes," she said, "if I have to!" Her face softened when she told me that the kewpie dolls she took were the only presents that her sisters got for Christmas, and she apologized for making me go with her.

It was as if that was the end of it for Bess. She would not say more, except to say that her aunt was a mean-spirited old witch and that she hoped their stay with her would be short.

All day I was so glad that Bess was back. Ivor did not come near me once. Bess made me laugh, imitating the way her aunt scrapes the butter off the bread if Bess spreads it too thickly. But I still do not like what she did, even if I understand now why she did it. It is wrong to take things that do not belong to you. You cannot say that it is right because you need something and cannot get it any other way. If Bess were right then we would not work hard like we do, we would just find a place to steal the money we need. It is our duty to look out for our families, but only honourably. Did I say I was the happiest girl alive, Diary? Well, I am happy but I am also very confused.

美

Bess is such a puzzle to me. Again she is act-
ing like nothing happened. She was jolly today,
and twice Mr. Hughes reprimanded her for giggling with Ada when she should have been copying from her history textbook. She may not like
her aunt, but I think that aunt is taking better
care of Bess and Declan than their mother did
— their clothes are clean, and Bess has stockings now, and new boots. Perhaps, yesterday, I
surprised her into the truth. I have thought long
and hard about this, and I have decided something. Bess is and always will be my friend. I
will keep her secrets, but I will not ever let
myself be drawn into something that is wrong.
There, it is written down, so it is for definite.

Miss MacDonald will not be back until next
week (which is just as well, Diary, as I have not
read her Christmas book yet. I have been so
busy!), so I am staying at the Lees' after school
each day until it is time to go to the restaurant.
Mrs. Lee is much stronger now, but it is nice to
help her prepare their meal, or play with the
children. I like the new baby. He has a face like
a little dumpling, and his arms and legs are so
fat that they have little creases instead of wrists

and ankles. Arthur does not like the baby. He says he is ugly and cries too much. I hope Sing-wah has a nicer spirit than Arthur. It will be strange to meet a brother who is already so grown. I long to see him.

### Friday, January 5

We have had another letter from Ma. It came yesterday and I felt too sad to write about it then. Baba has spoken to me today and now I feel a little better, but only a little.

She had it written three weeks after the last one, telling us that Grandmother is getting weaker, that she could not wait and would have to borrow some money to pay for a doctor and medicine. She would do this rather than sell one of our *mau-tin* of land. She said that she hoped that Baba had already sent the money and that it would reach them soon so she could pay the borrowed money back.

Baba explained that it takes time for such things to be arranged, that by now Ma should have received the money he sent. He reminded me how long our journey across the sea had taken, nearly three weeks. I could not help it — my lip trembled and my eyes filled with tears.

"Don't cry, Ah-Mei," Baba said, and with his thumbs he pressed away my tears from beneath my eyes. "Just wait, the next letter will tell us that all is well."

I do not question my Baba. Yesterday, though, I needed to know more, so I asked him how long it would be before we could send for Ma and my brother, Sing-wah. He sighed. "I do not know, Ah-Mei. Our savings mount but slowly; there is little left after we pay rent, and send money home." I thought of Bess then, of what she would do. Perhaps there was a more honourable way than hers. I asked if we could not borrow the money, maybe from a rich merchant like Mr. Mah. Baba laughed, then tweaked my pigtail. His smile at me was sad when he told me that the merchants would fear their money would not be paid back, because all we had to offer as security was our hard work, and in these difficult times with jobs scarce, that is just not enough. Baba's words fell into my soul like stones dropped into a well.

### Saturday, January 6

Oh, it was hard today to be cheerful. My thoughts kept circling round Ma's letter. I found keeping busy the best thing to be, that way pictures of them did not come into my head. I went with Mr. Chee to the Lees' after my chores, and played with the children a little.

Then I went to see Yook Jieh. I took my homework with me. I have to do a drawing, a drawing of a building. It is good that drawing is easy for me, because it is a subject that has to be passed, even for high school. I do not think this fair at all. Bess would never pass, even if she wanted to. All her people look like sticks with balloons for heads! I drew while Yook Jieh talked about the bachelors who are coming. Mr. Mah has said he is close to making a decision and she will be married by New Year. I hope it is a good choice.

Mrs. Mah has bought Yook Jieh some beautiful silks to make her wedding outfits. Deep, deep red for the wedding dress, and a lovely gold as well. Yook Jieh's fingers are skilful. I do not think I am being mean if I say that she is not a pretty girl, but these clothes will make her shine like a star!

Will there come a day, Diary, when I will sew like this? I do not know why, but my mind does not see it.

## Sunday, January 7

So many things have happened that I have become forgetful. At the end of last term I wanted to make a little gift for my teachers, but I did not do it. Now I have, and all thanks to Yook Jieh.

She leaned out the doorway today as I passed with Baba, and beckoned me in. Baba just smiled and gave me a gentle shove. I know he worries that I do not see enough girls my own age.

We had such a happy time! Her husband is chosen. His name is Cheung Wan-sheung. She has not seen him, but the Mahs tell her he is a good, hardworking man. I do not know how she can bear not seeing him until her wedding day. I know it is tradition, but it is so hard! I do not know this name, but I will ask Baba and the uncles. She will be his only wife, which is good. He has no wife in China. She was giggling, very excited about being the mistress in her own household. With a grand gesture she said, "Perhaps, *I* will have a *muui-jaai* to do my bidding!" Then her smile faded. She knelt down by her bed and looked at her sewing. I did not know what to say or do, so I sat and gently touched the silk scraps with my finger.

Yook Jieh asked if I wanted them. At first I thought to refuse, but then an idea came to me. I could use them for my gifts. My excitement showed and it was like catching a cold, because Yook Jieh got it too! She helped and now I have a beautiful red silk purse with little drawstrings for Miss MacDonald. Mr. Hughes was more difficult, but Yook Jieh showed me how to roll the hem and make a little pocket handkerchief.

### Tuesday, January 9

It is so hard to find time to write. Mr. Hughes keeps giving me more work to take to Miss MacDonald. The restaurant, too, is busy. Many bachelors come — they like Wong Bak's cooking because it makes them think of home. What is better, but scary, is that we are getting more customers from outside Chinatown. Wong Bak says they are working men so they have big appetites. This is good — big appetites means they spend much money. It is scary because unless Baba or Tsung Sook are there, I am the one who has to serve them. This is not proper, but what can I do? They joke and sometimes say things I do not understand.

How could I have not said before? My gifts were loved. I'm so proud that I can return kindness with beauty. I was very shy of giving the handkerchief to Mr. Hughes, but Bess kept prodding me until I did. He folded it there and then so that a neat corner stuck out of his suit pocket. It is a lucky colour. I hope it will be a lucky colour for him!

Miss MacDonald, I cannot believe that I have not written about her before now. Three days she has been back. I missed her a lot, because she is the person who understands how I feel about studying. For once she had no questions, just lots of stories about her brother's family. Her brother was a missionary in China, and Miss MacDonald would like to go herself. I did not know that she has been trying to learn Chinese. She asked if perhaps we may talk a little to each other in Chinese. This makes me happy to say yes, because this is another gift I can give. She loved my little bag, and said she would use it to keep her fob watch in when it was not pinned to her blouse. Today she smiled and patted my arm and said that she had something for me, but had not had time to unpack it until now.

She left and came back with a bag full of clothes. They are beautiful, clothes for a girl a little bigger than me, and boots, lovely leather boots. She told me that they were ones her niece had grown out of and wondered if I wanted them. Oh, Diary, I want them so badly, but I did not take them because I must ask Baba about such a magnificent gift.

### Friday, January 12

My eyes have stormed with tears so many times, but only when I am alone. No one knows that I am so sad.

Baba said no. He became as angry as I have ever seen him. He shouted at me, Diary, and threatened to forbid me to continue seeing Miss MacDonald. I was very frightened. I have not seen Baba like this since our first days in Gum Shan, the time of our return, when I feared he had become a crazy man. He shouted that Miss MacDonald was trying to buy me, and that she shamed him because her actions showed that she thought he did not provide for me as a decent father should. I became very small and still and my voice would not work. Mr. Chee joined in, saying that the foreign devils wanted our youth. Only Wong Bak spoke reason, and said that all he had heard suggested that she was a good woman, but just did not understand our ways. They are still arguing as I write, Diary. I do not want to write any more.

## Monday, January 15

I feel like I have been holding my breath. All weekend Baba was angry. He threatened to go talk to Miss MacDonald himself. I hid the book she gave me for Christmas because that might make him angrier still. I did not even write in you, Diary, because it might remind him of those who are foreign in my life.

I have been a mouse again, trying not to draw attention to myself. I've cleaned the room, worked hard in the restaurant, and said little. It worked. I was able to see Miss MacDonald today, but I may not accept the clothes. It rained so hard too. Those boots would have been lovely, but this is what must be.

Tsung Sook is the one I should thank. At the end of the clearing up yesterday, he started talking about Yook Jieh's betrothal and Cheung Wansheung. Baba did not say much, just muttered that perhaps the traditional ways were best.

My breath left my body then. I feared that Baba would forbid me even to go to school!

Tsung Sook's face went a deep, deep red. "Do you know Cheung Wan-sheung?" he demanded. "He is close to fifty, over three times that poor girl's age. He is a hard worker, that is true, but he is a skinflint. I heard him boasting how he will take Yook Jieh and they will go to a town in the prairies where there is no Chinese restaurant and that they will work there together to make a life for themselves and their children." He looked hard at Baba then, and added. "Think of that girl, she speaks no English."

Oh, Yook Jieh, my heart wailed, you had such fine dreams.

Tsung Sook was not finished. He looked at Baba and then at me. "Tradition is not everything, not here, and you have already shown you know that."

Baba did not speak to anyone all night.

This morning, as he left for work, he ran his hand over my head and said, "Study hard, Ah-Mei." Nothing more.

美

## Wednesday, January 17

Baba was very excited when he came into the restaurant tonight. Mrs. Baldwin had shown him in a newspaper that the great Sun Yat-sen has taken all of Kwangtung! Maybe now this will bring peace and Ma and my family there will be safer! I so hope that this will be true. Baba, Wong Bak and Tsung Sook had grins so big their faces would split. They all support Sun Yat-sen and his Kuomingtang. If we were able, Baba would give money like Mr. Mah and his friends. Only Mr. Chee grumbled and said that Sun Yat-sen was just another warlord. I do not understand all these politics, Diary, but I hope it will mean good things for my family.

Such excitement drove other thoughts from my head. Today I have been thinking about friends. Mr. Hughes set us an essay to write on what it means to be a friend. My friends, Bess and Yook Jieh, what would they make of each other, I wonder? Both are happy now, which is good.

What does Yook Jieh know about her bridegroom, apart from his name? She was a little tearful, so perhaps people have been talking. My heart ached when she said that she was lucky because Wan-sheung was a good provider, even if he was old. She patted my cheek, and laughed, saying that she was not pretty like me, so couldn't expect a handsome man. How will I get news of her? She can't read and write. I do not think that Wan-sheung reads English anyway. Oh, now my heart is truly aching.

Bess — Bess complains and complains about her aunt, but I think secretly she is happy. She has enough food to eat, her clothes are clean. Her mother has found a job, sewing in a factory, and once she has saved money then she will have the four younger children back with her. It is good to see Bess smile so much. She makes me laugh and lets no one get the better of her. I think this is good for me, because she says I am too serious for my own good. She tries to persuade me to hang around the schoolyard with her after school ends, but I tell her I must hurry to take Lily home and then go to Miss Mac-Donald's to study. Bess grumbles a little, but then she always walks part of the way with me. Lily loves Bess. We let Lily hold our hands and then swing her as we walk. Ivor has not bothered us, even though he walks the same way. Maybe he has forgotten me. He is very thick with a whole group of the other British boys and seems to be plotting something. I wonder what?

Such a to-do, Diary! Bess thinks my life is exciting. I think it is excitement that no proper person needs. I could not bring myself to write before now. I cried so much that my eyes were swollen. On Friday, at school, Ivor was mean about them, yelling, "No-eyes Chin!" instead of his usual insults. Even now my hand is shaking and it is difficult to hold my pen. It was dreadful, Diary.

On Thursday night I was alone with Wong Bak in the restaurant, because it was quite early. Three Canadian men came in, big rough men who swaggered when they walked, and pushed Mr. Chee aside as he hesitated in the doorway. They snapped their fingers and I went over. One of them did all the talking and he ordered so much food that I could not believe that three of them would eat it all. Wong Bak looked at me as if to say is this right, but what could I say?

The men ate noisily, shovelling the food in, calling me over all the time to fetch them more tea. I did not like them. I like them even less now. When they finished eating, they just stood up. Wong Bak rushed over with their bill. The one who talked laughed and took it from him, ripped it into tiny pieces and showered it on Wong Bak's head. I was so ashamed that they should treat him like this. I wished I was not a girl, that I was strong and could protect Wong Bak. I do not know where my bravery came from, but I spoke up. "You have eaten our food so you must pay us for it!"

They all laughed then, and the one who had ripped the bill said, "Ask the mayor to pay; he's the one who put us out of work." I did not understand this, and would have protested, but Wong Bak pulled me away. As they left one of them kicked over the little shrine by the door. That made me cry most of all. He had no need to do that. It was just meanness.

Baba and Tsung Sook were so angry when they came. Tsung Sook was all for going looking for the men, but Wong Bak would not let him. It was Baba who called the police. They came, big men with moustaches like dragon's whiskers. They had many questions for me. Sobs kept coming instead of words, and the policemen looked at me as if I were stupid. I tried and tried to describe the men. They wrote things down, but nothing will come of it. I do not know why Baba bothered. Sometimes I feel we are of no importance here. The police did tell us that the men were probably town workers who had just lost their jobs. Is that meant to help us? We lost money, money that would go toward our dreams.

### Monday, January 22

Yesterday Mrs. Mah shooed me away when I went to see Yook Jieh. She said that I would get in the way. This did not make me happy. I have felt very sour and hopeless, Diary, and then I do not like to burden you with it. Writing misery down does not make it better, it just makes me think harder about it. So I have been avoiding writing. I asked Miss MacDonald about whether or not I was being a good diary writer, as my entries no longer come every day like they did at the beginning. She wanted to see you, which shocked me. "Oh, not to read, May! A diary is personal and private. Just to see what type of diary you have," she said. I did not know that some diaries are made with the day's date for each day, and now I see that Miss MacDonald was worried that this was what was bothering me — big patches of dates with nothing filled in beneath them. She laughed when she saw you, and said that this was a journal in which I filled in the date when I wanted to write, so it was up to me to write as little or as much as I like. I am much relieved! She also said that many people start diaries and give up after but one week! She was very serious when she told me that sometimes writing down sad things helps you understand them. I am not sure she is right.

### Wednesday, January 24

Finally, something happy to write about. The Lees held a little party today to celebrate the fact that their baby, Charles, has survived one month. Many people visited, bringing gifts for the baby of clothes and money, or chicken essence to strengthen Mrs. Lee. I made Charles a toy out of my old blouse, the one Ivor ruined — just a little rabbit, one that a baby can hold easily. I also gave Mr. and Mrs. Lee a sketch that I had made of the children when they had all been listening to Mr. Chee tell them stories of the old railway days. I had helped Mrs. Lee boil and colour eggs to give away, and she had special cakes, coloured red, with a peanut filling. At the end of the party, she gave me many that were left. I will give them to Baba and the others, and there will even be ones to take for Bess and Miss MacDonald tomorrow.

I couldn't help it. I laughed loudly and I made Charles cry. I had forgotten that it is tradition to shave the baby's head the day after his party. When I saw him this morning, Mrs. Lee was holding him so just the tip of his head showed, and it was just like those lucky red eggs. Poor baby, he must be cold now, and he had such beautiful, thick hair. He likes my rabbit — Lily says he cries when anyone tries to take it away from him.

I wish I could say that Bess liked my cake gift as much. She was polite — her aunt is teaching her new manners — she didn't spit it out, but I could see she wanted to. Later I saw the rest of the cake hidden in her desk when she opened it.

I don't think Miss MacDonald liked it either, but she pretended that she did. She tries so hard to like everything Chinese that sometimes it is a little funny. I confessed that I find almost no time to read at home, so now ten minutes we spend reading *Anne of Green Gables* each day. Our lessons have a pattern: ten minutes where we go over anything I did not understand at school; thirty minutes on the extra work Mr. Hughes has set; ten minutes reading; ten minutes of Chinese conversation. Miss MacDonald is sneaky. In those last ten minutes she tries to ask her nosey questions. I pretend her accent is bad and that I do not understand!

### Friday, January 26

It has got cold again, and we have just a trace of snow. Disaster struck me! There, do I sound like Anne? I am laughing, but it is not really funny. My shoe has finally collapsed. Is that the right way to say it? The bottom part has been loose a little while now, and somehow, I don't quite know how it happened, as we were walking home Lily stepped on it, and now it flaps like a leaf in the wind. I was going to try and sew it together, but I did not have time before I went to Miss MacDonald. She was horrified, and insisted that I warm my feet by the fire. She went into another room and when she came back she held those beautiful boots, the ones that caused me so much trouble. "Just try them on, May," she said, "they may not even fit." Oh, but Diary, they did! Miss MacDonald sighed. "I understand your father does not like you taking things from outside your family" — that is the excuse I had made — "but this is an emergency. Would you like me to talk to him?"

That I did *not* want. So I said that I would speak to him. I put my old shoes back on, and as Baba and I walked home from the restaurant, the flap-flap of my sole could not be missed. I told him straight out, when he started to talk about buying some new cloth mary janes, that Miss MacDonald had offered me the leather boots of her niece again. Baba's jaw started to stick out, but I did not let him get angry. I explained how I was now helping her with her Chinese, and that if this was not enough, perhaps we could invite her to eat with us at the restaurant. I was such a daring girl, but, Diary, I so wanted those boots! Finally Baba said that if I wanted this so much, then it would happen. "You ask for so little, Ah-Mei."

I have my boots, but now I am not sure that it is a good thing that on Chinese New Year Miss MacDonald will be my guest!

### Sunday, January 28

Bess says that things, good or bad, come in threes. I now know it to be true. First there was Charles's baby party. Then I got my boots, and it was just in time, because yesterday we had a lot of snow! Now we have heard from Ma. Baba just read me the letter and Grandmother is better, not as strong as she used to be, but better all the same. Ma received the extra money we sent, and the medicine seems to have worked. My Baba swirled me up in his arms and danced me round our little room.

### Monday, January 29

Oh, it is lovely to have warm, dry feet. Bess admired my boots a lot. She still makes funny sayings about Miss MacDonald, but now she also seems a little curious. She asks me questions about her, how I spend my time with her. I wonder why?

It is good to have a friend like Bess to share things with and she was happy for me about our letter. She does not say much about her own family, but she did say that Liam visits now. I can be glad for her for that, because I know he is her favourite and she his. Declan is sour about it — he has not forgotten the beating that Liam gave him. When Liam comes, Declan will not stay in the house. I am sorry for Declan, it is true, but I do not like him. He is a boy with a mean spirit, who likes to tease and hurt. I did not like it when he clung to Bess, because even when he was miserable I had to watch him, for he would do nasty things to poor Lily as we walked home — trip her, snatch her little school bag or even pinch. She is such a sweet little girl, I do not understand what pleasure it would give him to harm her.

Declan does not stay with us much now, nor with the boys his own age. He is back with Ivor and his friends.

### Wednesday, January 31

No time to write yesterday. It was a big, big day for we Chinese. Consul Chow visited from America. Many, many men went to hear him speak. Baba was not able to, but Tsung Sook did. The Ambassador spoke against the schools in Victoria, praising the Chinese parents who have kept their children from them because the schools want to teach Chinese students separate from all others. I am very lucky that this has not happened here. I am one lucky, lucky girl. Tsung Sook was all fiery with protest, saying that our Ambassador would protect us, would fight against injustice for us. So did the many men who ate at our restaurant. Wong Bak just smiled sadly and said maybe so.

## Thursday, February 1

A month I have been free of him, but today Ivor started teasing me again. I think it is maybe Declan's idea. It is like I have been invisible for this time, and now he has remembered that I am here.

He noticed my boots, and made nasty comments about them. He even said I must have stolen them. I felt mad and ashamed at the same time. I do *not* steal. Bess yelled at him that a friend gave them to me, but he did not stop. He is such a clever boy, because he can turn anything hurtful. He called me a charity case, and said Bess was one too, that everyone knew that it was only her aunt's kindness that had kept them from the poorhouse. Oh, she was mad then and flew at him with her nails. I pulled her back because I saw a teacher looking at us, and I did not want her to be in trouble.

美

Miss MacDonald is very pleased with my work and that makes me happy. She says that in the last month I have made great progress, and that if I continue like this I could easily pass the entrance exam for high school. This made me happy, but sad too. She asked me today if I knew of other girls who might like to study with us. Bess, I said without thinking. Bess struggles with her schoolwork, even though I help her when I can. Miss MacDonald got very excited and wanted to know all about Bess, who she was, and why she had not seen her. "But you have," I told her. "She was the girl with me the very first day I met you, when we ran into you. She has blond hair and is taller than me!"

Poor Miss MacDonald. I had made her hopeful, and then thrown those hopes down. She seemed unable to say the words without tripping over them, but she explained it was Chinese girls she wanted to help.

Am I a disappointment to her because I do not mix with the merchants' daughters? My only Chinese friends are Yook Jieh and Lily — one will soon be gone, and the other is very little.

In my last entry, I said Yook Jieh will soon be gone, but my heart did not really believe those words. I am starting to now.

I spent the afternoon with her yesterday; Mrs. Mah did not send me away this time.

Yook Jieh's wedding will take place next weekend. It will not be fancy, but she is going to ask that I may be there with her. Cheung Wan-sheung will pay for a banquet to be held at the Mahs' house. The room he shares with his brother in Canton Alley is tiny, so it cannot be there. His brother and maybe one friend will attend, the Mahs, and me. The next day, Yook Jieh tells me, they will leave for Saskatchewan. Cheung Wan-sheung has opened a restaurant in a town there — I cannot remember the name. He and Yook Jieh will run it and soon his brother will join them. They will work to buy the brother a bride from China. I wanted to see Yook Jieh's face crinkle into a smile when she told me this, but it did not.

Baba and I stayed in our room this afternoon. We talked a little of Yook Jieh. When I said that I was frightened she would be lonely and sad, he sighed. "Ah-Mei," he said, "she may be, but she will have a husband, a business and then babies — let us hope she has many babies — to keep her busy. It will be better than any life she could have had if she had not come to Canada. I think you forget how hard life can be for people like us in China. Coming here, we work hard to make better lives, either for ourselves or for those back home."

That made me think deeply. I do forget, Diary. Life with Ma sometimes seems like a dream. My thoughts stay in the now and the what may yet come. Baba dreams of us here together, but does he also share the dream of so many here who work to go back to China and live the life of a rich man in their days of old age?

### Wednesday, February 7

Apart from Ivor's meanness, which I do not want to write about, life for me has been quiet. Nothing has happened, truly, Diary.

I spend my time with the Lees in the morning, and I am happy there with the children. Mrs. Lee is very kind to me, and even Mr. Lee is no longer grumpy. Yesterday he even called me Ah-Mei! The baby is growing, and he now has stubbly hair that sticks out like the feathers of a baby bird. When I hold him I picture Yook Jieh holding a baby just like him. How will she manage? Mrs. Lee laughs at my imaginings and says that Yook Jieh will be fine. I asked her what I might give Yook Jieh as a bride gift. I have no money to buy anything. I give all my wages to Baba. She said something to remember me by. I shall puzzle as to what that might be.

### Friday, February 9

The idea for Yook Jieh's present came to me yesterday as I was with Miss MacDonald. In the parlour in which we work there is a mirror on the wall. At the end of the lesson I asked Miss MacDonald if tomorrow I might use it to draw a picture of myself as I have no mirror at home. The idea amused her, and she asked if it was for drawing at school. I did not lie, but I did not tell the whole truth, either, because I did not think that she would understand about Yook Jieh.

So today, for most of our time, I drew. Miss MacDonald talked to me while I did, practising her Chinese. I did not know that she had trained as a nurse, and that is what she would like to do in China, be a medical missionary. That is a fine thing to do, helping others, maybe even people like my grandmother.

It is much harder to draw a picture of your own face than I thought it would be. I could not see what I was doing wrong, until Miss Mac-Donald showed me that I had made my face too round. She says it is more oval. I used pencil, and scribbled and scribbled to get my hair black. Watching me do this, Miss MacDonald asked why I did not use paint or crayons, and did I want to borrow some. It would have been easy to say yes, but I did not, although I did ask if I might use a red crayon she had to colour a fine, thick border around my picture. I was pleased because now I had framed my own face with luck. I hope it may bring luck to Yook Jieh.

When Miss MacDonald told me that I might have the makings of a good artist, my face was almost the colour of the border on my paper.

### Sunday, February 11

Yook Jieh is gone.

It is hard to write those words. I will miss her so very much. We had to snatch time to spend together, but what we did have was precious to me, and I hope to her. She was the one I talked to most about missing my Ma. She knew what it felt like; perhaps it was even harder for her.

The wedding was yesterday and Mrs. Mah let me be there, which made me happy. In fact, when Cheung Wan-sheung came to collect Yook Jieh, Mrs. Mah made me stand at the doorway with her and pretend not to let him in. She giggled like a girl and said that we could not fulfill all the traditions, but that one we could. He looked very old, Diary, but his face is not an unkind one. He laughed and went along with Mrs. Mah's foolishness.

Mr. Chee watched from the road. Later he told me he remembered Cheung Wan-sheung as a little boy, carrying water to the men as they worked on the railway. It is hard for me to picture that little boy. All I see is a man with a tired, weather-beaten face.

Yook Jieh was happy, but she cried a little too. There were smiles through her tears, and her cheeks looked like apples again.

She liked my drawing.

### Monday, February 12

I have felt sad all day. Bess said I was a misery guts, and spent recess with Ada. I did not mind, because I did not feel much like talking to anyone. I keep seeing a train in my head, carrying Yook Jieh through the high mountains to her new home.

I was lucky. Ivor did not bother me today. He and that group of boys still spend all their time huddled together.

## Tuesday, February 13

My heart came into my mouth today, because in all my thinking about Yook Jieh, I forgot some very important things.

At the end of our lesson today, Miss Mac-Donald asked me about celebrating Chinese New Year, whether we would mark it (I did not quite know what she meant here) on the evening before, or on Friday. Diary, I had not yet asked her if she would come and eat with us!

Why, I wonder, is that? Is it true forgetfulness, or is it because I do not really want her to come? It is difficult to explain. I do like her, but sometimes I find her very strange, and wonder what Baba and my uncles will think of her. I know that Mr. Chee will not like her, but he does not like anyone who is not Chinese. Will you think me sneaky, if I admit I did not think Baba would agree to her coming, that I just suggested it because I wanted those boots so badly?

I explained that we would eat very late, after my Baba was home, after we had closed the restaurant on Thursday. Then I asked if she would like to join us.

For a little while she said nothing. I wondered whether what I had asked might be an insult because she would be eating with strange men. But no, she smiled, a big smile that made her look almost pretty, that is if someone who has a nose like a bird's beak can ever be that! "Oh, May, I would love that. I would love to meet your father and tell him about what a wonderful scholar you are."

I am most unsure that this is good, Diary.

The other important thing I forgot is that tomorrow is a special day at school. It is Valentine's Day. People exchange cards, some-times in secret, sometimes not. For boys, it is if they want a sweetheart, but girls give them just to friends. I made one for Bess, because she is my friend, my only one now. It was very fine, if I say so myself. I coloured a red heart. Miss MacDonald let me use her crayon. Then I cut paper so it had a pattern of holes, like the lace on Miss MacDonald's blouse, and stuck this around the heart with flour-and-water paste. I hope Bess likes it.

### Wednesday, February 14

Bess is always a surprise to me. Just when we are getting back to being friends again, she gets cross over funny things. She is angry with me because of my invite to Miss MacDonald. I do not understand this. We are school friends. We do not go to each other's homes — well, I did once, but that does not count, I think, because I was not invited, just worried.

Bess walks with me to the edge of Chinatown, but she has never come in. People tell stories, not true stories, of what happens to white girls who come here. I said this to her, but she flounced her hair and said she did not believe such stories. I told her that our restaurant is small and that it will be very late, but she is still not happy with me. I do not know what I can do about this. It has had me thinking, long and hard. It is not like Bess, but I think perhaps she is jealous of the time I spend with Miss Mac-Donald. Of all the other girls at school, only Ada ever talks much to Bess, and that is only if no one else is there.

My valentine card was the only one she got. Perhaps that is also what made her sad and a crosspatch.

### *Sunday, February 18*

Oh, Diary, there is so much to write that I have saved it until I have a long time. Baba is sitting on his bed, carving a piece of wood he found, and I sit on mine, writing.

Thursday was busy, busy. I had explained to Miss MacDonald that I could not come to our lesson that day because the New Year must have a clean beginning, so our little room I scrubbed, and then I helped Mr. Chee with his, and there was still more, for Wong Bak and I made sure the restaurant shone before customers came. A lot came, which was good.

Canadians came down to watch the fireworks and procession with the fierce dragon dance. It was very fine. I saw many strange faces and some familiar ones too. Bess was there with Liam and his fiancée, but no Declan. She waved but did not come over. This made me happy but a little puzzled. Was she ashamed that I am her friend? I did not ask her at school on Friday. Perhaps the answer is one that would hurt too much. Declan I saw too, but later — he was with Ivor and a gang of big boys. They were running, jostling people and laughing. I shrank back inside the doorway. I did not want them to see me.

Our meal was also a good one. Wong Bak prepared many delicacies. I feared that Miss MacDonald would find them strange, but no, she tried a little of everything that I offered her — this was my duty as her hostess. I do not think she liked the whole fish. She shuddered a little when Wong Bak and Mr. Chee pretended to argue over who should eat its head. As oldest, it came to Mr. Chee, and he ate it with much lip smacking! My mind could not be still through this time. I watched Miss MacDonald and Baba and my uncles and no one was at ease — not even Baba, who works each day for a lady who is very like Miss MacDonald. Talking was little, and very polite about things that do not matter. Miss MacDonald asked some questions about where Baba and Tsung Sook worked, but Baba's answers were very short. She went red, and talked of China instead and her plans to go there. There were many silences and I felt too shy to fill them, especially when Miss Mac-Donald praised me to Baba, telling him that my school work was very good. That was the only time my Baba smiled that night. I am happy to have made him proud.

Today we have talked of New Year and Miss MacDonald. I was filled with flutters of fear when Baba started this talk, fearful that he did not approve now that he had met her. She does make him uncomfortable, that I see, perhaps because she *is* very bold, but he told me that I am lucky to have been befriended by her. This made me calm inside. My time with her is a jewel in my day and I would not like to lose it. He only asked me to beware a little, beware that she might make grand plans that do not allow for who I really am. I do not understand what he fears.

Oh, it is nearly time to leave for the restaurant, and I have not told of my great good fortune. I am a rich girl. On Friday I was given *two* lucky red envelopes with money in them! Baba I knew would have one for me, though it pained me to think that it is money not saved. I told him so, and tried to give it back, but he just smiled and closed my hand over it. Then when I took Lily home after school, Mrs. Lee gave me one too. This I did not expect. They each had a 25¢ note in them! I shall think hard on what I might buy. Perhaps Bess will have ideas.

Bess had so many ideas that my mind is whirling. My 50¢ is not enough to buy clothes, but Bess told me about 1¢ sales at the Rexall. Can such a thing be true? What would I buy? I could maybe buy little things, as gifts for the people I love: for Baba I would buy a book, maybe from the White Lamb bookstore. Oh, and maybe I could even buy a toy, just a small one, for my brother for when he and Ma come. Ma is difficult to choose for, but a nice bar of soap might please her. Bess had one idea that made me feel very excited — the cinema! I have never been to the cinema and I would love to go. Bess hasn't either, but I hear the others at school talk about it, and it sounds like magic — to sit in a big, dark room and be whirled away to another place or even another time by the pictures on the screen. Bess tells me that children are ten cents to get in. If I could go I would take her too. I would share my good fortune, and still have money left to buy treats for others. Is this an impossible dream? Will Baba allow such a thing?

## Wednesday, February 21

I wish Bess had not put the cinema in my thoughts. It is like a light that shines all the time. I want to see it so badly. After our lessons today I asked Miss MacDonald about it. My cheeks felt hot, because she did not understand me, and thought I wanted her to take me! I explained that no, I had money from New Year and wondered if it was a suitable thing for me to do. She laughed and said that she didn't see why not, as long as I didn't see something trashy. I do not know what trashy means. She looked in the paper and told me that *Oliver Twist* was playing. I know *Oliver Twist*. This is a book we read in class. There was much in it I did not understand.

Miss MacDonald said it would not be good to go alone, and smiled when I told her that if my Baba let me go I would go with Bess, perhaps this Saturday. Miss MacDonald is very kind, and asked if Bess and I would take tea with her after. This would be very fine for both of us.

美

We are going! I asked Baba carefully, telling him that the film was of a school book, and that I would go with a school friend. He did not even think much. This surprised me. He said that if I was careful and respectful then I may go. My face must have showed my surprise, because he explained that my life was in Canada for now and it should move beyond Chinatown, if only in little ways.

Oh, Bess was excited. She grabbed my arms and whirled me round when I told her in the schoolyard. Ivor saw and made snickering noises but we ignored him. When I told her of Miss MacDonald's tea invitation, I thought she would burst she was so happy.

There was one bad thing. Bess did not mention it until the end of the day, almost like she did not want me to have time to think and say no. Her aunt does not like the boys Declan has been hanging around with, and is making him spend much time with Bess. She wanted to know if he could come too. Am I a nasty girl? I think maybe I am. I said yes, but it burned my heart to do so, to spend my good fortune money on him.

## Sunday, February 25

Again I saved a big time to write. My eyes are still round from what I saw! The cinema was beautiful, with red velvet seats and curtains. There were gold painted angels on the walls. Bess and I were almost silent. Our tongues would not work in such a place. Declan did not come. He was with Bess when she met me, but ran off, yelling that he would meet Bess again at 5:00 on the corner of the street of their aunt's house. I did not want to stop him, but suggested to Bess that we should. She shrugged and said that he would be off with Ivor, that they were building something on some vacant lot. I soon forgot about him.

When the lights went out, I nearly shrieked, because a lady playing a piano popped up through the stage! I did not know why she was there, but when the film started, it all became clear! She played music to go along with what happened in the film: sad music for the sad scenes, frightening music when something bad happened to Oliver. Poor Oliver had such a sad life.

Tea with Miss MacDonald was fun too. I asked Bess whether her aunt minded her coming to tea, because of the stories about Chinatown. She laughed at me, which made my feelings sad. Diary, she did not ask permission! This is very shocking, and I told her so, which made her laugh again. "Oh, Mei-ling," she said, "why would I ask her something that I know she would forbid, going into Chinatown and having tea with a missionary? We're good Catholics, she'd have seven kinds of fits!" All through tea Bess was happy and she made Miss MacDonald laugh with all the stories she told. She ate a lot!

When it was time for her to leave, Bess thanked me, and asked whether we might do this again next week. I made her sad, I think, when I told her that the rest of my money was for gifts for my brother and Ma.

### Monday, February 26

I told Mrs. Lee about how I was spending my red-envelope money on gifts for my family, when I dropped Lily off today. She asked me if I knew when we would send for Ma and my brother. I had to say no, not for sure. She took my sadness at this away, because she said that I would make Ma proud when she came. I do not like to bother Baba, but I wish he would talk to me more of this. I have given him the money I earn, and I hope it builds a little at a time with our savings.

Miss MacDonald was funny. She told me how much she had enjoyed meeting my friend, but that we were chalk and cheese. She had to explain that this meant we were very different, and she wondered aloud how we had come to be friends. I explained to her how Bess had looked after me right from the beginning of my time at school, and that Bess had few friends before me. This seemed to mean something to her, because she said, "Ah," in a funny way. I was a little offended, Diary, because she then said Bess was rough around the edges. I do not think it nice to make opinions like that. I think she saw, because she added that Bess's life had obviously been harder than most, but that deep down she had a good heart. Of course she does!

### Tuesday, February 27

I tried to talk to Baba about when Ma might come, but he was tired, and brushed aside my questions like he would an annoying gnat. All he would say was that it would happen; he promised me that. I do not like to pester, but I do miss Ma, and it seems to become deeper lately. I think it is seeing Lily and Mrs. Lee together. I watch her braid Lily's hair and remember Ma's quick fingers twining mine. I feel hollow inside when I see them together — a hollowness that sometimes does not go away easily.

At school, something is going on, but I do not know what. It feels funny. It is the boys, they look at each other strangely, but say nothing. I asked Bess. She did not know, but said that Declan was being very secretive, and that their aunt is worried about the times he disappears for hours on end.

### Wednesday, February 28

I cannot get Ma out of my mind. I hate it that I don't know how she is or what is happening in the village. I wish there was a way that my thoughts could reach her, or that I could talk to her. Baba writes every month when he sends money, and I know he tells her of what happens in my life here. Her replies are so short — often just two lines, saying that she has got the money and that they are well. Sometimes, only sometimes, she will add that she has used the money to buy another *mautin* of land to work. Is this because she has to tell the schoolmaster what to write down? Is he impatient with longer letters, as he has to write them for many families? Or does Ma not like to share our family news with him?

### Thursday, March 1

A new month, Diary, and have you noticed that I have been dutiful in my entries. I hope this will continue. I will have more schoolwork than usual, though. It was very exciting today, because Mr. Hughes announced a contest.

A former pupil has visited from Ontario, where he now lives. Mr. Hughes was his favourite teacher, the one he says who helped him most. He wants to encourage us to work hard, as he did when he was with Mr. Hughes, and he has set an essay competition with two dollars and a dictionary as the prize. We are to research and write about either the land we came from, the place we live now or any province of Canada. We may use illustrations if we wish. Our entries must be in by Friday, March 23rd, and the winner will be announced a week later, but on the Thursday because the Friday is the Christians' holiday and there will be no school.

What a grand idea! I would love to win, but I do not think I will. Everyone was talking about it. Ivor boasted that he would win because he would write about Britain, which as everyone knows (*he* said), is the greatest country in the world! I have not decided what I will choose, but I will enter, that is one certain thing. Bess grumbled and asked Mr. Hughes if we all had to enter and looked very cross when he said we did.

I forgot to mention that the dictionary is very beautiful. It has a black cover with gold letters. Mr. Hughes has put it on a shelf behind his desk, facing us. "To inspire us!" he said. I am inspired, but I think more by the $2.00 than the dictionary!

### Friday, March 2

I learned a new word today, "blustery." We have strong, strong winds, a little rain and snow. Mr. Hughes described the weather as blustery. I like the way the word sounds. You can almost hear the wind in its middle.

I have felt very tired all day, and when I was with Miss MacDonald the numbers of my Maths problems spun around the page and would not stand still. I did not tell her this, but struggled on. I do not think I want to write any more — my head feels funny. Baba is waiting to put out the light.

Diary, I did not forget you, I was just sick. My head is a little clearer, but it still hurts. I have had a big, big fever with aching bones. I do not remember much of Sunday. Baba says that when he came home I was very hot and lay in my bed all limp. Mr. Chee had sat with me, but when Baba arrived he was relieved because he was just going to get Mrs. Lee, as I was not making sense when I talked, mixing English and Chinese together.

People have been very kind. Mrs. Lee has sent soup over with Mr. Chee, and a message from Lily that she had told Bess what was wrong with me. On Monday I was too sick to even remember that I should go to Miss MacDonald. She came looking for me. It was lucky she went to the restaurant and found Tsung Sook there, who told her what was wrong. If she had come to our room, I'm sure that Mr. Chee would either not have answered her knocks or would not have let her in if he did. Tsung Sook spoke to Mr. Chee and told him that Miss MacDonald would visit me on Tuesday and that he should be sure to let her in. Mr. Chee made a sour face, but he did. While she visited, he stayed, sitting on Baba's bed, glowering at her.

I thought that she would be angry with me for not coming, for missing our lessons, and that she would make me do them there and then. But no, she felt my forehead with her hand, and shook her head, saying that I was still feverish. She said I probably had the influenza that was going round. She had brought me some lozenges to suck for my sore throat, and then she sat and read to me. We finished *Anne of Green Gables* and she brought another Anne book yesterday. I shut my eyes and let the words flow around me. For just one little moment I thought my Ma was there, smoothing my hair from my forehead, but when I opened my eyes, it was only Miss Mac-Donald's hand.

### Sunday, March 11

When I wrote on Thursday I thought I was feeling better, but the sickness came crashing down on me again, like a waterfall. All I have wanted to do is sleep. Never have I missed a whole week of school before. I hope I have not fallen too far behind. Miss MacDonald has told me not to worry, that we will catch up quickly if we work together. She has been very kind, coming every day and spending some time with me.

She too brought me soup to eat, something she called consommé, that she said was good for invalids. I did not like it, but I ate it. It was weak tasting with a funny perfumey taste. Miss Mac-Donald said that was sherry. I like Mrs. Lee's chicken soup with ginger much better.

We talked about the essay competition this morning. I still did not know what I wanted to do. I would like to write about China, but I do not know its history, not its grand and proper history — just bits of stories and legends that Baba and Wong Bak have told me — and surely that is what an essay like this will expect. So, I thought instead, I would write about Ontario, using the books we have in school. Miss Mac-Donald sniffed a little at that and said that this would just be copying, as I have never been there. She thought to write about China would be much better, and it didn't matter that I didn't know the history of the whole country. I should write about my village, where it is, what it's like, what stories and legends are told about it. When I thought about it, I liked that idea more and more. I can draw pictures from my memories: my grandfather working the fields, my grandmother sitting on the porch telling Little Brother the stories she once told me. My eyes feel wet as I think of them, wondering if she makes him the little clay figures she once made me. I wish I could hear those stories again. Does Sing-wah realize what a fortunate boy he is?

Baba just came back from the restaurant. He is very happy that I am now truly feeling better. He told me that my uncles had missed me. I missed them too! The only one I saw was Mr. Chee, who watched over me so well this week. Perhaps he is not so much an "uncle" but a "grandfather" — a grandfather who is sometimes a little crotchety, but one who is part of my Gum Shan family here. He poked his head round our door this morning, but when he saw Miss MacDonald there he grunted and went away. I had thought he might come back this afternoon, but he did not.

### Tuesday, March 13

I went back to school yesterday, and it was very hard. My head still is buzzy inside, and even just walking with Lily there left my legs feeling like they had no bones inside. A lot of students have been sick. Ivor has been absent these two days. Bess seemed pleased to see me, which made me happy. She taught me a rhyme about my sickness, which made me laugh.

*I had a little bird whose name was Enza,*
*I opened a window and in flu Enza.*

Then she told me how the rhyme came about — how in 1918 many, many people got sick with influenza and even died. The rhyme showed how easy it was to catch it — people believed just by opening a window and breathing the bad air. That was not so funny.

Mr. Hughes gave me all the work I missed to take to Miss MacDonald. Yesterday she thought I looked too tired to do much, so we talked — talked a lot about my life before I came here. I am getting used to Miss MacDonald's questions now. She is just a very curious person.

Last night I did not write, my body wanted to sleep so hard. Today I feel a little stronger.

## Wednesday, March 14

Ivor is still away. Is it wicked to hope that he will be sick as long as I was? He has not done a big mean thing to me since my blouse, but when he is there, I must always be watchful. It is not just me who feels like this. It feels better in class without him. It is hard to explain, but the funny feeling that school had — a feeling like something bad was going to happen — is not there when he is away. Only Declan misses him, and that is because the other bigger boys, Ivor's friends, do not have much time for him.

### Thursday, March 15

Please forgive my short entries, Diary, but I am working on my essay for the competition at night, when I normally write in you. Miss Mac-Donald has been very kind and given me paper to use, and has lent me crayons. Our village is so small that I could not find it on a map in the big atlas she has, but I have drawn a map of Kwangtung province, showing the district of Poon-yue, and explained that it is there. It is making me happy and sad to do this. Happy because I am thinking of the good things that happened when I was a little girl. The sadness comes because I want to see my Ma so badly. I think that she might not even recognize me now. I have grown so much taller.

Baba has watched me work, and it is funny because I have to explain things about the village to him. This puzzled me a lot because I thought he should know these things. Then he reminded me that he left when he was just a little older than me, when Uncle Wing-lok sent for him, and that he has only been back twice in all that time — once to marry Ma, and later when he brought me here. I wanted to ask him which was now home for him, China, where he was born, or here, where he has lived so much longer.

### Friday, March 16

Ivor has been absent the whole week!

Bess showed me her essay. It is done, she says, and that is that. She only worked on it in the time Mr. Hughes gave us in class. She drew a map of Ireland, and copied things about it from a book. I tried to help a little, suggesting that she might add some more details, or even correct the words that she had copied incorrectly. This did not please her, and she tossed her hair and got huffy. "Not everyone is a swot like you, Mei-ling," she said.

I did not like this, but then thought that perhaps I had hurt her feelings. Bess tries to make it seem like nothing bothers her, but I know things do. I have seen her cry.

美

My heart is full with worry. Mr. Chee has not been well. It has felt frivolous to worry about you, Diary, when there is so much to be done.

All last week, his cough — the one that never really went away since last year — got worse. Yesterday when I went to help him clean, he was still in bed. His face had little drops of sweat upon it and was very pink. I did not know what to do. Baba had already left for work, so I could not ask him.

While my mind thought, my feet had ideas, and I found myself running to the restaurant. I knew Wong Bak would be there, or in the room above it where he and Tsung Sook sleep. I ran so fast that I did not hear the men who called out: their faces and voices were lost in the air.

Wong Bak came at once. Since then, either he, Tsung Sook or Baba have been with Mr. Chee. Wong Bak sent me to buy herbs, which they brewed as tea to ease Mr. Chee's sickness. Then he sent me to the restaurant, and this has stolen all my time. We have managed, but it has been hard. Tsung Sook and Baba do not cook as well as Wong Bak. One rowdy table complained, and Tsung Sook was very angry. He told them not to come if they did not like the food. I thought they would fight, but it did not come to that, thank goodness. One man asked where Wong Bak was and I told them. They grew very silent. Everyone knows Mr. Chee.

Last night, Baba slept on the floor in Mr. Chee's room. Wong Bak will sleep there tonight. Tsung Sook tomorrow. I will be helpful in any way I can. I hope that Mr. Chee is well soon. That silly rhyme that Bess taught me about my illness keeps going through my head.

### Monday, March 19

Ivor was back today. He had influenza too, but perhaps not very badly. He boasted how his mother had brought him his meals in bed, and how she went to the library for him and got books so he could finish his essay. He made a great show of handing it in early to Mr. Hughes. It did look very fine. He had made stiff covers for it and covered them with wallpaper — white paper with raised patterns on it, he called it anaglypta. I looked at Bess, and said that he would probably win. She thought so too, and said that he would be very smug and unbearable if he did.

I had to stop writing. There was much shouting and I heard Tsung Sook's voice, so I went to see what was wrong. He was struggling with Mr. Chee, who was trying to get out of bed and calling for people whose names I did not know. I helped Tsung Sook get him back beneath the covers. I was scared because Mr. Chee's eyes did not seem to see us. I sat on the side of his bed and held his hand. He grew calmer, the shouts becoming little mutters. Tsung Sook's voice was shaky when he thanked me. He said I had a knack for nursing.

When Baba came home, I asked him if it is my fault that Mr. Chee is ill. Baba said that perhaps Mr. Chee might have caught influenza from me, but that he could have caught it anywhere, as many people have had it. Lily Lee did not go to school today and, at Baba's job, both boys have been home ill. This only made my worry go away a little.

## Tuesday, March 20

I have finished my essay too. I worked on it in class a little, and then took it to show Miss Mac-

Donald. She read it while I worked on some Maths problems. It was odd because she sniffed as she read it, and her eyes were teary.

"Oh, May," she said, "it's beautiful. You must miss your family so much."

I told her that I do, but that here it is good too, because I am with my Baba and that one day we will *all* be together. That is something my Baba says will be for certain. Miss Mac-Donald looked sadder then, and she hugged me, saying, "Oh, I hope so, May. I do hope so."

### Thursday, March 22

I try so hard to write each day, but some days there is no time. We are all very tired. Tending to Mr. Chee fills the time more and more. He is not eating and his fever does not break. We are all worried.

Last night when the restaurant closed Wong Bak came home with us to spend the night watching over Mr. Chee. He and Baba talked in low voices, I think so that I would not hear, but I am ashamed, Diary, that I strained my ears to catch their words. Baba thought that we should seek treatment for Mr. Chee. He wanted Tsung Sook and Wong Bak to take him to the little hospital run by the white nuns on Keefer Street. They take in men who are sick and have no family. Wong Bak would not agree. He was very fierce, more fierce than I have ever heard him before. He argued with Baba, telling him that Mr. Chee would hate that, that it would frighten him, and that *we* are his family. It made me scared to hear them talk like that, as Baba would not suggest such a thing unless he thought Mr. Chee to be very, very sick. Wong Bak did bring a herbalist to see Mr. Chee today. I hope the medicines we bought will help, just like the medicine helped my grandmother when she was sick.

### Friday, March 23

The herbs do seem to have helped. Tsung Sook said that Mr. Chee slept more last night, and did not just toss and turn. His breathing is very rattly though, and he still does not want to eat much. Tonight I sat with him so that Baba and Tsung Sook and Wong Bak could be at the restaurant; Friday is a busy night. Mr. Chee slept mostly, but once he woke up, looked at me and called me by a girl's name that is not mine. This made me sad as I wondered who that girl had been — a wife, maybe, or a daughter?

I gave my essay to Mr. Hughes today. I could not make a beautiful cover like Ivor's, but I drew a picture of our village for the front. Ivor saw it and laughed rudely, asking loudly why I had drawn pictures of sheds. Mr. Hughes spoke sharply to him, but he did not seem to care. He was strange all day today, as if he were excited about something. He kept whispering in class to his friends, and at recess a big group of them were all bunched together again. A lot of the Italian boys were also standing in a group in another corner of the schoolyard. Bess asked Declan what was going on, but he stuck his tongue out at her and told her to mind her business.

My study time today was not good. I have nearly caught up with all my work, and I thought that Miss MacDonald would be pleased, but she did not seem as if her mind was with me today. I asked if perhaps she was not feeling well, but she said that she had many things to think about. It was very strange.

### Sunday, March 25

My eyes are sore from weeping. There is a hollow space inside me. Mr. Chee died on Friday night. Wong Bak was with him, and that was fitting — they have known each other many, many years and come from the same village, a village close to ours. It is hard, Diary, my words are muddled when I write. I write as if he is still alive.

I spent much time with him, but I knew very little of his life. Instead, I listened to his small grumbles of how his bones ached — one foot had been crushed working on the railway — of how strange Canadians were. He did not talk of family, and never went back to China. Little jobs kept him, and kindnesses from those who had known him a long time. He always ate with us at the restaurant, and in return was often my guardian when Baba could not be with me, especially when I first came. His friendship with Mr. Lee's dead father meant that he was welcome to spend his days in their store, drinking tea and playing a little *mah joong* on the tables at the back. Many stories have been shared since Friday, and more will come when we have a banquet to honour him. Baba and the uncles will see that all is done properly. They have already contacted the association of the people from our district and the leader will attend. They will also ship his bones back to China when it is time.

I cannot write any more.

## Monday, March 26

The banquet to honour Mr. Chee will take place at the end of the week. I do not know that I will be allowed to attend, some may not see it as proper, but I will help with the preparations.

It was hard to make my mind behave at school today. Mr. Chee was in my thoughts and it felt like I was shut behind glass windows. People talked to me and I could not hear them. I told Bess what had happened, but she was a good friend, she let me be in silence. No one bothered us. Too much else was going on — much whispering, and many of the boys have bruises and cuts. Bess said there had been a big fight on the weekend at some vacant lot. Declan was boasting about how Ivor had led them and that they had given the Italian boys a beating that they would not forget. I did not care about this. It is just spitefulness. I was glad when the day ended and I could walk Lily home. She was quiet too.

## Tuesday, March 27

It has been a little better today, but only a little. Mr. Chee is still much in my thoughts. I talked of him to Miss MacDonald. She was very kind, and did not mind when I cried. She talked about her church and how they would say that Mr. Chee had gone to be with god. Miss Mac-Donald has talked of her god before, but not much. Today I had to ask more. Mr. Chee did not believe in her god, so how could this be? She explained that this did not matter — that her god loved everyone and that, from what I had said, Mr. Chee was a kind and good man. It is very puzzling. She asked me if perhaps on Sunday I might like to attend church with her. She thought it might make me feel better. I do not know. Baba's hero, Sun Yat-sen, is a Christian. So it might be all right. I would not lose time with Baba as church is in the morning, so perhaps . . .

School today did not help my thoughts from sadness. All day the boys in our class were niggling each other, that is the word Bess used. Ivor all the time made remarks about how the Italian boys cannot fight, and made faces at them. They were all angry at each other, and Tony Sarducci punched Ivor in the back of the head as he walked past his desk. Mr. Hughes was very furious and sent him to the principal. It did not seem fair to me. Ivor, who is the cause of the trouble, did not get punished. That is how it always is though. He is too sneaky to ever get caught.

## *Wednesday, March 28*

A dreadful, dreadful day. I am even sadder, because I may have lost Bess as my friend and I may have made new enemies. I do not think I can bear this. She and I have argued, and, of course, it is about Ivor. Why does that boy make so much trouble?

At recess this morning I did not feel well. My stomach was not settled, so I asked if I might go inside. It was permitted, but Bess was told she could not come with me. I could hear voices in our classroom, and when I peeked around the door, I was surprised to see Tony Sarducci and another boy there. They were standing by Ivor's desk and laughing. This was strange, but I did not think too much of it, and went on to the cloakroom to sit quietly. They did not see me.

Later, when our lessons started, Mr. Hughes's face was very white, and he would not allow us to talk. He pointed behind his desk, and told us that the dictionary prize was gone. It had been there before recess, so someone must have taken it. I felt scared because I had been inside

— would he think that it had been me? He made us all stand up and open the lids of our desks while he came around and looked inside. When he got to Ivor's he reached inside and pulled out the dictionary. Its beautiful cover was ripped, and pages were falling out and torn. Ivor's face went very pale and he started to cry, saying that he did not know how it had got there. Mr. Hughes did not listen. He just took Ivor by the arm and marched him out of the room. No one spoke. Then the noise came. Some people, and Bess was one, were laughing, happy to see that Ivor was in trouble. I did not say anything, but I remembered Tony and the other boy.

When Mr. Hughes came back his face was very stern and Ivor was not with him. I did not know what to do, so at lunch I told Bess what I had seen. "Good for them," was what she said. "It's time someone took Ivor down a peg or two! They're just getting their own back." When I told her that I thought I should tell Mr. Hughes, she got very angry and said I was stupid, here was my chance to pay Ivor back for all the mean things he had done to me.

Her words hurt.

Ivor was back after lunch, his face all red and

wet with tears. The principal had given him the strap.

I told. I thought and thought, and then I told. At the end of the day, when I went to pick up work for me and Miss MacDonald, I told Mr. Hughes what I had seen. Now I worry that when Bess finds out she will not be my friend. I also worry that others will hate me too. Did I do right, Diary?

### Thursday, March 29

Such a sad entry yesterday. It was hard to write.

I did not want to go to school today as there were so many bad things to face, but I had to take Lily and that was an end to it.

My worst fear was not a true one. Bess came straight up to me and said, "You told Hughesy, didn't you, Mei-ling?" She shook her head, so her hair bounced. "I knew you would, you're such a goody two-shoes!" Then she grinned. "Not like me," she added. "I would have let him suffer."

I was very scared in class, but Mr. Hughes did not say anything at all until the end of the day, when he put our essays on his desk, and began a long, long talk about how sad he had been that such meanness had come into our class, leading to the destruction of one of the prizes. He had much else to say, but my heart was beating so fast that I could not hear, until I heard Ivor's name and that someone had tried to make him look like the thief. I shut my eyes tight as Mr. Hughes continued talking, explaining that the true thieves had been caught and punished. He did not say it was me who had told! I was so happy that I almost missed hearing who had won.

Ivor won. There were groans at this, but Mr. Hughes glared till there was silence. Two other essays were mentioned as being very good and mine was one of them!

At the school gates, as Bess and I waited for Lily, Ivor came by. He was on his own. He stopped and stood for a long time, but did not speak. He looked very uncomfortable. When he left Bess snorted and said, "He knows that you saved his bacon! What a toad he is — couldn't even bring himself to thank you."

I did not mind that. I am much relieved that things are right. Now, this weekend we will say goodbye to Mr. Chee.

美

It was strange not to go to school yesterday. I had thought that there would be much time to write, but it was not to be. It is also strange to be writing now, in the morning. This is time that I would be with Mr. Chee.

Even though there are many people in this rooming house, I feel very alone now, especially when Baba is at work. I will fill this emptiness by writing of yesterday.

All my thoughts were of Mr. Chee, even when I spent the morning helping Mrs. Lee. She talked fondly of him, laughing about the way that even when he was not playing *mah joong* himself, he could not resist watching others, and sometimes criticizing them if he thought they made a stupid move.

My afternoon was all chopping, chopping and slicing for the banquet. The restaurant closed after lunch, so that we could prepare. Wong Bak looked tired and sad, his back more bowed than usual. Tsung Sook was very solemn. He talked much to Wong Bak about the future, how he wanted to make sure that he married and brought a wife here. I knew he was thinking of how lonely Mr. Chee's life here had been. Wong Bak made Tsung Sook smile, reminding him of how Mr. Chee teased him that a tall, good-looking man like him would find a very grand bride!

Many came — old friends from the railway days, Mr. Lee, members of the district association, and even the Mahs' cook. This made Wong Bak nervous a little, but I was happy to see Cook as he had news of Yook Jieh. Her husband had written to say that they were settled and the restaurant open. How I wish I could write to her, and her to me!

Wong Bak's food was very admired. He had put much effort into it. He cooked and then Baba and Tsung Sook made him sit while they carried the food to the table. I stayed in the kitchen, washing pots and, should I be ashamed to say, listening.

It made my heart full to hear the talk of Mr. Chee, making me feel a little that he was still there. But, oh, Diary, I became angry at them, the men who were there, because soon the talk changed. They started to talk of what was happening in China, of how Sun Yat-sen had lost control of Kwangtung, and was imprisoned on a boat. They talked of things happening here, of how bad things are, how things may get worse.

This scared me and I wanted to hear more, but Wong Bak silenced them, reminding them of our friend who is gone.

In what way could things change and become worse for us? I must find out.

### Sunday, April 1

Baba would not answer my questions last night. It was late. He was tired. It was nothing to worry about, just foolish talk. That was all he would say. This has not calmed my worries, but made them worse.

I could not think who else to ask, and then it came to me — Miss MacDonald. She had asked if I would like to attend church with her today. It is a special day for the Christians, Easter Sunday. I went. I put my cleanest blouse and skirt on and walked to the church. Without Mr. Chee I felt very alone, but he would not have approved of me going there, I know. I shut my ears to the shouts of the men.

I had seen people walk to church many times, but did not really know how many came — it was very full. I crept into the back, quiet like a mouse. My eyes searched for Miss MacDonald, and I saw her near the front, sitting with some other white women. I saw Mr. and Mrs. Mah there too.

It was hard to follow the service, but I stood and sat when the others did. Some of the songs I knew from school. A man spoke for a long time, talking about how Easter was a time of things becoming new again. At least, that's what I think he said. Their god died and rose from the dead, and promises eternal life in heaven for all people. I hope for that to be true — for Mr. Chee. My head was hurting though, it was all so strange, and I was glad when it ended.

I waited while people left, and was going to make my way to Miss MacDonald, but she came to me.

"Oh, May! You came." Her face was full of smiles. "Did you like it?"

I did not know what to say. I was not thinking to like it. Perhaps my face was sad, because she put her hand on my arm and asked me if something was wrong.

I did not hesitate, but told her what I had heard.

Her smile went and she shook her head. "I think, May, that your guests may have been talking about something that is taking place in our Parliament."

Parliament I know. Mr. Hughes has explained the government of Canada to us, but why would Parliament try to make life harder? I asked this, saying that Parliament is to make life easier for people in Canada.

"Let's sit down, May," Miss MacDonald said, and she led me to one of the church's wooden benches. "Some people have introduced a law that will change the rules about how Chinese people can come to Canada, to try to stop so many coming."

"But why?" The words burst out from me so loudly that people turned and stared. I tried to make my voice obey, but it would not. It continued to shout. "Chinese people are hard workers. We only want to make better lives for ourselves, here or back home in China. Why would the government want to stop us doing that?"

Miss MacDonald reached out and tried to put her arms around me, drawing me closer to her. I shrugged them off. "It's complicated, May," she said, "but I want you to know that I think this proposed law is wrong."

I could not listen. I could not hear. My heart was loud in my chest. I wanted to cry out, "Ma!" I did not. I ran. I pulled away when Miss Mac-Donald tried to stop me. I did not listen to the words she was saying as she ran behind me. The street was crowded, but I did not care. I pushed and shoved my way through, ignoring the curses that were thrown after me. All I wanted was to be gone, to be safe inside our room.

I cried and cried, big sobs that hurt, with many tears. I don't understand why this is happening. Why people want to hurt us.

### Later

I was crying again when Baba came. I did not want to be so, but my thoughts were filled with fear. He thought it was for Mr. Chee.

My words did not have steadiness as I tried to explain. It took a long time for Baba to understand, and for a while he just held me while I made his chest wet with my tears, a blotch the shape of my face on his shirt.

"There have been rumours, Ah-Mei," Baba said, "but there are always rumours of things like this. It will come to nothing. Perhaps it will even be good for us. Some say that the head tax will be abolished." He pushed me gently back, his hands on my shoulders so he could look into my face. "Now, would not that be a good thing? We could send for Ma and your little brother immediately, and still have money to send to Grandfather to hire men to work our land, while we all work here!"

Baba was smiling. When he smiles, he does not look so tired. I tried to smile back. Baba is very wise. He must be right. I do not think I could bear it if he isn't.

### Monday, April 2

No school again, so I had much time by myself, as Mrs. Lee did not need me. Some time to think, and some to make things right.

The making right was with Miss MacDonald. I was very rude yesterday, not listening to her. I know that she spends much of the day in the Mission, so I went there this morning, hoping. She was sorting bundles of clothes with some other women in the big hall. I did not like to disturb them, so I stayed quiet, waiting.

It did not take long until she saw me and ran over, looking more and more like a heron with her long legs and awkward running. She was smiling and her arms were out like she would hug me, so my fear of her anger went, especially when she asked me if I was all right. At first I stood stiff, but it is nice to be hugged, to have someone care for your feelings.

Miss MacDonald excused herself from the others and offered me lunch, saying that we could talk and eat. It was good and she explained much to me. Like Baba, she thinks that this new act of Parliament will probably not come to pass, or at least not as it is written now. She said it is born out of fear and misunderstanding. This I did not understand so well, until she explained that in hard times, times when there are few jobs, people fear for what they have, and it is easy to blame those who are different, like us Chinese. That made me very sad. We are not different, not deep down — we care for our loved ones and want to make good lives for them. Why is that threatening?

After lunch she asked me whether I would like to help sort the clothes. They are clothes they have been given to send to China. I was very shy, but Miss MacDonald insisted. It was not so bad. The other ladies did not speak much to me, but it was interesting to hear them talk of their plans for raising money for missions to China, and even of their families.

When I returned home, I had a big scare. I heard noises in Mr. Chee's room and thought that it must be either Wong Bak or Tsung Sook.

We had cleared the room yesterday — he had very little — but perhaps they might have come back to clean more. I went in and a strange man was sitting on the bed, a man who yelled at me. I ran away very fast.

### Wednesday, April 4

School is good. Ivor has not bothered me at all in two whole days. He even smiled at me once. Bess said that maybe he is *sweet* on me, and laughed wildly. I ignored her. She thinks she is very funny, but she is not. Ivor is a much quieter boy at school these last two days. Even Declan says that he is no fun. I think this is good.

Bess has been a funny mixture, happy one moment, and sad the next. Her mother has not been able to work. She too has the influenza. Bess fears that she may lose her job. If this happens, Bess says that she will get a job and bring money in to help her aunts look after them. I told her that I did not think she could, that she is too young. She just snorted and said that I earned money. I did not think that a Canadian girl would have to do this.

美

Today is Sing-wah's birthday — my little brother is three years old. I wonder what he looks like, and how he spent this special day. Do Grandmother and Grandfather make much of him, as they did me when I was there? I would think so. My grandfather had many praises for me, telling me how clever I was. Sometimes he would sigh, and say that if only I were a boy I would have a magnificent life. I think that is why he so wanted me to come with Baba to Canada — maybe I could do great things here.

I do not like to talk much of my family, but today I did, telling Miss MacDonald all about Little Brother. She had many questions, asking whether we would bring both him and Ma together. "That is our dream!" I said. "But maybe, if we cannot save money fast enough, we would just send for Ma."

This shocked her very much. "But who would look after your brother?"

I thought this to be a very silly question. It was obvious that it would be my grandparents. We would still send money and they would pay men to work the land, until we could all be together.

## Friday, April 6

I do not like it when people argue. It makes me feel all twitchy inside.

The new act, "the legislation" is what Miss MacDonald calls it, is all that people talk of now. I hear snatches of conversation on the street, and in the restaurant, angry voices reach me in the kitchen. Even Wong Bak, Tsung Sook and Baba talk of it, and it is their arguing that scares me and makes my thoughts troubled. Tsung Sook is very fiery. He is convinced that this will end all Chinese coming to Canada for-ever. His voice rises and he tells the others of things he hears, or things he reads — details of what is proposed; how, yes, the head tax will be abolished, but how new rules will be made so only very few, very special Chinese people may come to Canada. My heart felt close to breaking, because Ma and Little Brother do not fit that description, except to me and Baba.

Tsung Sook dismissed Baba and Wong Bak's arguments that the Canadians always propose things like this, but that they will not happen. He was very angry. In fact he did not stay, but left, saying that he would go to his Clan association, where they were not pretending that nothing is happening, where they are talking about what they can do. It left a taste like bitter melon in my mouth. Baba and Wong Bak talked long of this, saying that Tsung Sook was young and hot-headed.

I do not know who to believe. Will Baba listen to my fears?

## Saturday, April 7

I do not like Saturday any more. Without Yook Jieh and Mr. Chee it is a lonely day, with long hours to fill. The man who now lives in his room is not a nice man. He scowls at me whenever he sees me. I think it is because Baba has spoken to him twice when he came in late at night, stumbling and cursing loudly.

As soon as my chores were done I went to the restaurant. I feel comfortable there with Wong Bak. He talks more to me now, and I like listening to his stories. He has been here even longer than Baba, coming when the railway was first being built — over forty years ago. I thought he might think it rude, but I asked him why he had no wife. He smiled and said that he had one once, but she died when there was fever in his village, and he had never been able to afford to marry again. That made me sad, but Wong Bak smiled and told me not to waste my tears. He would return one day to the land that his money had paid for over the years, and which his brother's family worked. He would be the much-honoured uncle from Gold Mountain.

Tsung Sook did not come to work in the restaurant today.

## Sunday, April 8

It was a rainy day, so when Baba finished work we stayed quiet in our room this afternoon. It was good, because we talked.

Baba had many questions about school, about how my work progresses, and about Miss MacDonald's help. He seemed pleased by my answers, smiling a little and nodding. He made my heart full when he told me how proud he was of me. Baba does not waste words, so these were jewels to me.

He seemed in so much of a good mood that I dared to ask him things — about our life here, and life at home in China. I did not think he would answer me, and might get angry, but he did not. He came and sat on the chair under the window, by my bed. His words were slow in coming, but now I understand more, I think of the dreams he has for us. Of making life easier for his parents with the money we earn here, and of a new life, a Canadian life, for me and Sing-wah, where we will live in a country not bound by old ways. A country where even though the Chinese are not always welcome, we have big opportunities.

Baba's eyes were not looking at me as he spoke. He stared at the wall and then he was silent. I did not like to break the silence, but I wanted to tell him of Wong Bak's dream of going back home to China, and know whether this was how Baba's dreams ended too. My question startled him and he shook himself like a dog coming out of water before he answered.

"Home?" he repeated. "Where is home for me, Ah-Mei? I have lived here so long, I don't know anymore."

### Tuesday, April 10

Since Ivor has become so quiet, school is a peaceful place for me — a place to work hard. I do not need to be watchful all the time. Bess has been away for the last two days and, before, this would have been a big worry for me. I would have felt very alone, and maybe even a little scared, but not any more. Ada and some other girls talk to me more too. I feel shy with them, but they do not seem to mind.

At home it is still a troubled time. Tsung Sook did not come for three days to the restaurant, which meant much work for us all. He left for his work on the docks early in the morning, and did not come home till very late. Wong Bak waited for him to talk, to find out what was wrong, but Tsung Sook would not talk until last night. After the restaurant closed, he, Baba and Wong Bak sat and drank tea. I sat in the corner, doing my homework for Miss MacDonald, but listening too.

Tsung Sook is a good talker, but his words make the worry in my heart wake up. He does not share Baba and Wong Bak's belief that this new law will not pass. He thinks they are being foolish. He told them that there are meetings where people are getting together, that they should come, that it is necessary to fight the passing of this law.

They did not say they would go, but their faces were serious. I tried to talk to Baba of this as we walked home, but he said that it was not for me to worry, that I should not listen in to conversations. I am becoming scared again, Diary. I wish there was someone I could share my fears with that this law will stop Ma and Little Brother from coming.

## *Wednesday, April 11*

Bess is back. I tried talking to her, and now I feel worse, especially as I was mean, very mean, to her.

Perhaps it was not a good time. Bess was out of sorts. Her mother did lose her job, and Bess spent Monday and yesterday trying to find work for herself, but did not. Her aunt is very angry with her, because Bess was meant to come to school on those days. Declan told on Bess. Her aunt has said that the family will rally round. I think this is good, but Bess was grumpy.

While I told her of what Tsung Sook had said, she twiddled the ends of her hair and sighed. Her words came out fast, interrupting me. "Liam says that maybe this law is a good thing."

My mouth fell open, but I could not speak. How could Bess say that? I stared and stared at her, willing her to take those words back. Even now, I do not know whether I was hurt, angry or maybe both. I know I wanted to take Bess by the shoulders and shake thoughts like that out of her. She did not see me then, just kept talking. "After all, it's the Chinese workers who make it difficult for the rest of us, Liam says, because they work for less pay!"

I could not help it — tears came to my eyes, but no words to my mouth still. Bess looked at me then, and told me not to cry, that she didn't mean it personally, she was just repeating what her brother had said, and of course she would like for my family to come, but . . .

I did not want to hear her buts, Diary. I did something I have never done before. I turned away and left her standing there. I walked over to the far corner of the schoolyard and turned my back on her. I did not speak to her for the rest of the day, no matter that she tried to make me.

I am just so sad because if Bess, who is my friend, thinks this, what must *others* think?

### Sunday, April 15

I have not written, Diary, because I have felt so sad. I did not want your pages to be tear stained. Bess's words, said so quickly, have stayed in my heart. I feel like there is no hope if this is how people feel, no matter how many Clan association meetings there are.

I do not think that Bess even knows how hurtful those words were, and I could not tell her, not without crying again. Ignoring her did no good. Day after day she just kept talking and talking to me like there was nothing wrong, until it was just easier to answer. She was back to her normal self, cross with Declan for telling on her, cross with her aunt for being such a fussy person, but pleased a little too, perhaps, because all the fussiness means someone cares about her. Sometimes she does not seem to see other people's feelings.

Money is being raised to fight the law. Each person in Chinatown is being asked to pay a dollar, each business to pay two. There is to be a big concert at the Sing Kew Theatre in Shanghai Alley. Lily Lee is going with her father and Arthur. She asked me if I would like to come, but I did not want to ask Baba for more money. I asked Tsung Sook what they will do with these funds they raise. He said that they will send business leaders, important people, to Ottawa, to the government, to persuade them this law is wrong.

美

I do not think that I have been a good student for Miss MacDonald, this last little while. It has been hard to concentrate with my thoughts so fixed on Ma. Miss MacDonald has been very patient, not saying anything until tonight, when I was not paying attention as she explained some Algebra to me.

"For goodness sake, May!" she said. "Are we both wasting our time here?"

My face was very red. I felt very ashamed. I put my head down on my book so I did not have to face Miss MacDonald. She has been giving up her time for me, and now I repay her with this. She very gently raised my face so I had to look at her. I did not mean to, but I told her of what Bess had said, how those words had wounded me and scared me.

She was kind. She is always kind to me. I like that she talks to me like I am not a child. She did not lie and say that what Liam thought and Bess said was just one opinion. She told me that many, many people think like that, and that many, many people do not even think at all about such things. Her church does not want the law either, and they will speak against it. They think that life would be easier if Chinese men had their families here. Then there would be less gambling, less opium smoking. Her Mission also has Chinese ministers who would not be able to come to Canada under this new law.

As we spoke my heart felt lighter, but now, as I sit and write this, it becomes heavy again. A church is a powerful thing, but is it more powerful than the voices of those many, many people Miss MacDonald mentioned?

### Wednesday, April 18

It was hard to find time to write last night. Baba and Tsung Sook went to one of the meetings that Tsung Sook had told them about. That left just me and Wong Bak to work. My fingers are red from washing dishes, and it was late by the time we got home, because we had so many customers.

Tsung Sook was smiling when he and Baba came back, but Baba's face was not. He was pale and tired looking. He had no smiles for me or for Wong Bak. I wanted to hear what had been said, but Baba said it was time for me to go home and that he would walk with me, then return to the restaurant. I wanted to stamp my feet, I was so angry, but that would not be the way of a good daughter. Baba did not come home until very late. He crept in, putting on no light. This morning he was gone early too. I wanted to ask questions before he left, but the look on his face changed my mind.

I wish I knew what had been said!

## Thursday, April 19

I am so happy. No, happy is not a big enough word for how I feel. I should have known that my Baba would take care of things! He is sending for Ma. He is watching me write this and smiling. I am sure he knows what it is I am telling you, Diary.

When I got to the restaurant after my time with Miss MacDonald, I knew that something had happened, but I did not know what. Wong Bak kept giving me funny looks and smiling, smiling like he had a secret. It was nice, but annoying — nice because it is truly the happiest I have seen him since Mr. Chee died, annoying because I wanted to know what it was that had made him happy!

When Tsung Sook came, it was obvious that he knew too. I almost could not stand it, Diary, the long, long wait until Baba arrived. Even then they did not tell me straight away, but waited until we had few customers left.

The meeting two nights ago is what did it. Baba said that people were arguing over how to fight the law; they could not agree. This did not make him hopeful. He has decided that we must do something now, not wait. We have enough for the head tax for Ma — Baba stroked my hair and said that my earnings had helped with that — but not for her steamship passage. For a little minute, this worried me, but his voice was happy and there had been so many smiles that I knew there would be a solution. Wong Bak is lending us the sixty dollars more we need. He is such a good friend!

Baba is not trusting this to a letter. He will send a telegram tomorrow. It will still take time, because Ma will have to be told of it, and then reply, travelling maybe even to the city to do it. But this will be maybe a week or two, not months.

I cannot wait to tell Miss MacDonald tomorrow. She will be happy for me, I know. Bess too. I will forgive her those thoughtless words.

美

## Friday, April 20

I was right about my friends, their happiness was great. I told them as soon as I could. I told Mrs. Lee in the morning too. The news burst out of my mouth like a bird taking flight. I could not stop it.

Bess did not say much, just grinned, but she knows how much this will mean to me, how much I have missed Ma.

Miss MacDonald was very silly. She grabbed my hands and danced me around the table in the parlour, until we were both out of breath. Her silliness made me even happier. "This calls for a celebration!" she said. "Let's forget about work for today, and let me take you out to tea!"

I would have liked that very much, but I could not go. Wong Bak was expecting me. Miss Mac-Donald would not be put off. She insisted that we will go tomorrow instead, and have tea like a pair of fine ladies.

## Saturday, April 21

I feel like I am floating on a cloud and nothing can bother me now, not even the nasty looks the waiter in the Hotel Vancouver gave me when

Miss MacDonald took me to tea there. She noticed too, and told me to ignore him, that it was his ignorance showing. I have never been to such a beautiful place before, and it was hard not to stare. My skirt looked shabby and worn against the silk of the chairs, but I do not care about that now. Clothes do not matter, when my Ma is coming.

Miss MacDonald had many questions about Ma, and I tried to answer, but some I did not know the answer to, like whether she would want Miss MacDonald to help her learn English. One question though, made my happiness go a little, and made me feel very mean and selfish because it was something I had not given one thought to, not once since Baba first told me the good news. Miss MacDonald asked how long did I think it would be until my little brother could come too, and who would travel with him when he did.

Does my happiness come at the expense of his? I think it must. He is little, and I have never met him, so it is easy to forget. He will just come later, that is certain. Baba has promised. Being left is not that hard; he will still have grandparents to love him.

## Sunday, April 22

Baba and I went to Stanley Park this afternoon. There was no rain and the air was mild. I like the hollow tree, hiding inside, but today we walked and walked by the sea, making many plans. With Ma here, she can cook alongside Wong Bak, and Baba says that my help will not be needed so much. He looked slyly at me, smiling. "Maybe high school will not be just a dream, Ah-Mei," he said. My heart was so full that I thought it might burst, and it was hard to listen to the things that Baba added about the difficulties I would still face, the ones that come from people not liking the Chinese to be here. He would like to leave the Baldwins, and maybe seek work on one of the boats, as a steward or cook. The money is better. Tsung Sook has been talking of doing this too, but Baba could not do it unless Ma were here to be with me.

It is good to have plans and not worries.

## Monday, April 23

It is so hard to be patient now. I want the telegram from Ma to come so badly. Once it does, Baba will book her passage, and in maybe a month or two she will be here.

Bess says that I am giddy with happiness. She laughed to see how happy I was, and said that a whole new Mei is appearing — one who giggles and smiles a lot. This is true, but I would not giggle like she does in class, not ever, and especially not now. I must study even harder.

Not many of our class will go on to high school when we graduate in two years. It is much work and hard examinations to pass. Ivor probably will. He is a clever boy, and maybe not such a mean one now. He has not teased anyone for so long. Others do not tease or pick on him either, though. They know that he has a temper. There are some Chinese boys too, who will go to high school, some of the merchants' sons. I think I might be the only girl with such high hopes.

### Thursday, April 26

I have not written for a while, Diary, but this is not because anything bad has happened. I do not wish to bore you, that is all. How many ways is it possible to say how happy a person is? Or to write I wish the telegram would come?

Miss MacDonald has much praise for me. She says that I am working very hard, even harder than I used to. I worried that she might think that now I do not need her help any more, because I like the time I spend with her so much that I do not want it to stop. She wants me to meet some of the boys who study English at the church — one in particular, who is already in high school, and who is going to Toronto to study. I do not know about this. I shall ask Baba.

There is no good news about the law, just much talk that it will pass the House of Commons soon. This scared me some, because I thought that it would stop Ma from coming, but Tsung Sook explained. He reads the Chinese newspaper and speaks with others. It will not become a true law until it is passed in the Senate, which it has to do as well. There will be months or even more time before this happens — time for Ma to come, time for people to still keep fighting against it and stop it.

美

## Saturday, April 28

Still no telegram!

I have nearly filled you now, my beautiful diary. I want to keep pages so that my last entry in you can be made on the day I see my Ma!

I spent much of the day with Miss Mac-Donald. It makes the long day pass quicker. I do not think so often of Mr. Chee. I drew some pictures that she will use at Sunday school with the little children. She asked me if I would like to help with this on Sunday mornings; some of the littler ones do not speak much English, and I could translate for them. She smiled and said that I could learn some more about the church too. I think I would like that.

## Sunday, April 29

I enjoyed helping out with the little children at the Sunday school. It was not hard. Lily and her brothers and sister were there, all except the baby. I drew pictures with them and listened to bible stories. Miss MacDonald gave me a bible of my own to take away and read. Perhaps I will, perhaps I won't.

Afterward when people stayed and talked,

many were fearful that their families would suffer big separations if the law is passed. Miss MacDonald smiled at me. I knew what she was thinking. I was thinking it too — my time of fear is past.

### Thursday, May 3

I thought I could do this, but I cannot. Ma is not coming. I

### Sunday, May 6

Oh, Diary, what am I going to do? Every time I try to write about how I feel, the tears come. They are there now, prickling at the backs of my eyes. I have cried for days, ever since Ma's reply telegram came. It said very little, other than she could not come now, that Baba's parents could not be left and that the time was not a good one.

Baba's eyes were wet too, when he told me, but he did not seem angry, or even surprised. I am the angry one. As I listened to him talk, trying to explain why Ma would make this choice, that this was a delay, not a final thing, I could not bear it. He had many reasons: how she was fulfilling her duty to his parents; how she could not leave little

Sing-wah; even how she might have heard stories from those who return which would make her think that coming to Gold Mountain was to come to a scary, unwelcoming place.

These are just excuses! But what about *me*, I wanted to shout. *I* am here. Does that not mean something to her? Has she forgotten me? Are Baba and I less important to her?

Baba did not sound like himself, but he tried to make his voice strong and smooth as he told me some silly story about the Old Man of Yu who one day decided to move the mountain in front of his house so that he could get to market more easily. People laughed at him and said that he was wasting his time because he was too old to accomplish such a huge undertaking. In turn, he laughed back at them and said that when he died his sons would take over, and then their sons, and when they died, as they must, their sons would complete the task.

This is nonsense, just a story to placate a child. It means nothing to me — it has nothing to do with Ma and our family being together.

I feel like a wild girl, wild with the feelings that rage inside me. I shouted at Baba. He was trying to calm me down, telling me again and again that our family would be together some day. "Some day is not good enough!" I shouted. "I want my Ma now."

Then my words were unforgivable. Just as Baba used an old story, I used a proverb. Now I wish I had not. My words cut Baba like they were stones I threw at him. "Just remember," I told him, "for a girl to grow up without a mother, is to grow up no better than a worm!"

## Monday, May 14

It is worse when people are sad for me — it makes me cry more. School is good, because Mr. Hughes did not keep on when he asked if something was wrong, and I said no.

Bess — Bess is trying to help. She says things like, "Your dad's right, Mei-ling, it will all work out one day." This is not a help to me. How far away is that one day? If that stupid law is passed that one day might be never! At recess I go off by myself and sit in the cloakroom. I thought it would be a place that no one bothered me, but I was wrong.

My head was on my knees, but I knew someone else was there. When I looked up, it was Ivor. He was just staring at me. I waited for his meanness to come out, but it did not. Finally he reached into his pocket and brought out a handkerchief. His movement was jerky as he thrust it to me.

"You should wipe your eyes," he said. His voice was stuttery, like he was scared. Then, just before he turned and ran away, he whispered. "I'm sorry, May."

### Tuesday, May 15

Those words I said to Baba have not been mentioned, but they hang between us. I want to apologize, to tell him that my life here with him is a good one, but my hopes of seeing Ma soon — the hopes that have been broken and flung aside — make my apologies stay inside me. I do not yell any more, nor stamp my feet. I still do not understand Ma's choice. It is a choice that cuts me deep inside.

But it is not fair to blame Baba. I do little things. I make sure that tea is ready for him in the morning. I sponge his jacket clean. I make him eat before he starts work in the restaurant. I think he knows how I feel. His eyes are sad when they look on me, but he pats my hand.

美

I used to complain that Baba did not talk much to me of plans and important things. Now it is as if he talks too much. Each night he and Wong Bak sit me down and say soft things to me, telling me that things will work out eventually. That we will continue to work hard and in two, three, maybe even ten years we will have money saved, enough money to bring everyone. That if the law, the one they are calling the Exclusion Act, is passed now, there will come a day when it will be changed again. "Hah!" is what I say in my head to their words. I do not say that aloud. I cannot forget the look on Baba's face when my other cruel words wounded him.

Miss MacDonald is the one whose words comfort me most. Her words are not apologies or ones that soothe. Instead she says I must make plans, must work hard, do well, and perhaps this will enable me to find a way to see my family again. She will not say exactly what she means, but there is a sureness in her words that lifts my heart a little.

I have only three pages left now, Diary. I will save them, and the last one will be for the day I see my Ma again.

### Thursday, June 7

A letter came from Ma, addressed just to me. Baba offered to read it to me, but I did not want that. I keep it tucked inside my blouse.

### Sunday, July 1, 1923

I am using one of my precious pages to write on Dominion Day. Or should I say Humiliation Day. That is what it is being called in Chinatown. All the talking and protests came to nothing. That horrible law is passed.

No more ordinary Chinese will be allowed to come to Canada, and that would include Ma and Sing-wah. I can write that calmly now, Diary, because I am no longer the wild, sad girl who wept on your pages. Some days I still am, but those days become fewer and fewer. I can't give a name to how I feel always.

I finally opened Ma's letter. Miss MacDonald gave it to one of the Chinese-born missionaries and he translated it for me. How could I have doubted that Ma loved me? Even in the formal flowery language of the scribe who wrote it for her, her love shone through. She wrote about things we had done together, how she still keeps my baby shoes and clothes, holding them tightly to her when she thinks about me. She told me how she cried for days when Baba's telegram came, because she knew that she could not come, that Grandmother was too frail to look after Sing-wah. My tears matched hers as I read her plea that I persuade Baba to bring me back to her, her belief that we could be together back in China, that we would manage somehow.

My heart leaped at the idea, but I knew that it could not be, even without talking to Baba. His life is here now, whatever hardship it brings. He has lived here so long that our tiny village would be strange to him. His dream is of a life here in Canada for us all, and I know that he will never give that up.

I understand his story now — the story of the Old Man of Yu. I will not give up either, because I am part of that story. It is Miss MacDonald who will help me do my part. It will be much work, but I will never falter, and our family will be together again no matter how long it takes.

美

### Friday, March 29, 1935
### Kwangtung, China

I am very good at keeping promises. Today I saw Ma and my little brother, although perhaps I should not call him that. Sing-wah is fifteen, and taller now than I. Your pages are getting tear stained again, Diary, but these are special tears — tears of happiness.

Ma and Sing-wah came from the village to the mission headquarters to see me before I set off to the clinic, a journey that will take several days. We talked long into the night.

Ma was beautiful in my eyes, frail but beautiful. How hard these years of separation must have been on her! At first she was shy, and did not say much, just stroked my hair, and ran her hands around my face. Sing-wah was not shy. He had so many questions for me, most of them about Baba and Canada. I gave him the photographs I had brought with me and he stared so hard at them, I thought the paper would catch alight.

When it was time for them to leave, I made them many promises: that while I am here we will see each other as often as we can; that we will make up for the lost years. The most important promise I made many times — that I will work and work to bring us all together one day!

# *Epilogue*

美

Mei-ling *was* good at keeping promises.

Life in Chinatown after 1923 was not easy, but Mei-ling and her father chose to stay and continue to work hard in the hope that some day their dream of reuniting their family would be fulfilled. Mei-ling did indeed go to high school, as did Ivor. They never became friends, but Ivor never again teased and persecuted Mei. Bess left school as soon as she could, and she and Mei drifted apart.

The relationship Mei-ling had established with Miss MacDonald became more important to her, with Miss MacDonald becoming in some ways the mother she missed so much. It was with Miss MacDonald's encouragement and the help of her church, which Mei-ling attended regularly, that Mei-ling was able to take up a scholarship to study medicine at the University of Toronto — something that was not possible at that time in her home province of British Columbia. Upon qualifying as a doctor in 1935, Mei-ling went as a medical missionary to China. For one brief period, she and Miss MacDonald worked alongside each other until ill health forced Miss MacDonald to give up her dream of working in China.

Mei-ling and her father always kept in touch with her mother and Sing-wah, either through friends such as Wong Bak, who returned to China for good in 1928, or through letters. It was this that allowed Mei-ling to arrange for them to visit her on her arrival in Kwangtung in 1935.

The Japanese invasion of China in 1935, and the subsequent war, led to great turmoil in China. Mei-ling came back to Canada in 1939, fearing that she would be trapped in China if she did not. She settled in Toronto to practise medicine. Her father and Tsung Sook joined her there and set up another restaurant, like the one they had previously owned, although this time it was Mei-ling's father who did most of the cooking. Tsung Sook had gone home to China in 1928 — the same year Wong Bak returned to stay — and married. The restaurant that he continued to run on his return to Vancouver in 1930 enabled him to send money to his wife and the son she bore him.

During the Second World War, communication with China became increasingly difficult. For a period of five years Mei and her father heard nothing from her mother, and did not know where she and Sing-wah were or, indeed, if they were alive. In 1946 they got word from Hong Kong, where Mei's brother, now twenty-six and married with small children of his own, had found work in a factory.

Mei-ling never gave up hope that the family would be reunited in Canada. At the expense of having much of a personal life, she put her considerable energy and determination into working with other Chinese people to change the hated law which did not allow Chinese to bring their families here. When the act was repealed in 1947 it appeared that her dream would finally be realized; but even then her patience was tested, for although her mother came in January of 1949, it took much longer to bring her brother and his family to Canada. The whole family was finally reunited in 1953. They had five years together before Mei's father died at the age of seventy one.

Mei's brother, having spent most of his life working on the family land, and speaking little English, did not find it easy to adapt to life in Canada. But he worked with his father in the restaurant, taking over his share on his father's death. His dream was that his children, and their children in turn, would gain an education and make lives for themselves in Canada, just as his sister Mei-ling had done.

Mei-ling did not marry until quite late in her life, since her main goal was to ensure that the family was settled in Canada and financially secure. She married a fellow doctor in 1959, when she was forty-nine. Having no children of her own, she was a devoted and much-loved aunt to all her nieces and nephews, encouraging them and helping them achieve their dreams.

Mei-ling never lost the habit of keeping a diary. Her diaries became family treasures after her death in 1988, when they passed to her great-niece Elly Chin. Elly followed her aunt's example in many ways. One of those was becoming a doctor. Another was keeping her own diary. Here is an extract from one of Elly's diaries:

美

## March 2003

It was so cold today, even though the sun was shining. I was really worried about Grandfather. He is getting so frail now, and standing around in the cemetery was not the best thing for his cough. He wouldn't listen to me, though, just laughed when I suggested that he stay at home. He teases me that ever since I qualified as a doctor, I think I know everything, but I know he is proud of me and doesn't really mean it. He's never missed Ching Ming, not since Great-Aunt Mei died. He says that it is the least we can do, on this day of remembering our ancestors. For the first time though, he was not the one to clear the twigs and leaves from her grave — that fell to my father and his sisters.

Grandfather stood nodding, holding my arm. His eyes were wet with tears, and his voice raspy as he turned to me and said, "You know your Great-Aunt Mei came and found me in China, don't you? Gave my mother and me such hope that we would come here? Always honour her, Elly." He gripped my hand hard. "Promise me you will. She worked so hard and gave up so much to bring us all together."

I couldn't speak for crying, but I squeezed his hand back and nodded.

# Historical Note

美

Canada is a land built on the work of many immigrants, who travelled from all over the world to settle here. Chinese immigrants have been coming to Canada for over two hundred years, and today there are flourishing Chinese communities in most of Canada's large cities, notably Toronto and Vancouver.

Many thousands of Canadians are descended from those first immigrants, who crossed a wide ocean, often living away from their wives and children for decades, hoping to build a new life in what they called Gold Mountain. In cemeteries all across Canada, Chinese families gather to honour their ancestors when Ching Ming is celebrated, reflecting on their lives and what brought them to Canada, and respectfully sweeping the gravesites clear.

The first record of Chinese immigration to Canada is in 1788, when Captain John Meares anchored two ships in Nootka Sound on the Pacific coast. His task was to build a settlement, and among his crew were fifty Chinese carpenters and craftsmen. Little is known about what happened to those fifty men after the settlement was built. Some records indicate that there was an attack by Spanish forces which resulted in the destruction of buildings and the capture of many of the settlers, who were taken as prisoners to Mexico. Other stories have some of the Chinese carpenters avoiding capture and intermarrying with the native people of Nootka Sound.

The first large-scale immigration of Chinese men to North America came with the discovery of gold, first in California in 1848 and then in the region of Canada's Fraser River ten years later. They worked as miners or labourers in the gold fields. Most of the immigrants came from Kwangtung (now called Guandong) province in China, and were seeking to make a better life for themselves and their families who, for the most part, stayed in China.

British Columbia was the place where most Chinese immigrants settled. A vast province which was still relatively underdeveloped, it lacked the manpower to undertake the tasks necessary to settle the area. Chinese workers filled that need. By 1863 a thousand Chinese labourers were working on the Cariboo Wagon Road leading to the gold fields. Western Union employed five hundred Chinese labourers to string telegraph wire between Westminster and Quesnel in 1866. Chinese and Japanese immigrants also worked in developing industries, such as the fish canneries that were built on the coast of British Columbia.

The construction of the Canadian Pacific Railway was the event, however, that brought the most Chinese men to Canada. The final section of track through the Rocky Mountains to Vancouver was built during the period 1881–1885, using the labour of as many as seventeen thousand Chinese men. The conditions they worked and lived in were often harsh and primitive. It is said that one Chinese worker died for each mile of track that was laid.

Although the Chinese were needed for their labour, they were often resented by the white population alongside whom they worked. They were seen as alien and very different in their habits. One accusation that was often thrown at them was that they were "sojourners" who had no intention of making their homes in Canada, and who came just to earn money to send home. Unlike immigrants from countries like Great Britain, who were encouraged by the Canadian government to come to Canada, much was done to discourage Chinese workers. Once the railway was completed, no provision was made for the Chinese men, who struggled to find new employment. They were viewed as a problem by the governments of both British Columbia and Canada. In an effort to stop further immigration, a head tax was introduced in 1885. By law, each Chinese immigrant had to pay a tax of fifty dollars in order to come to Canada. This was far more than many Chinese men already in Canada were able to save from their wages, after paying for food and lodging and sending money home to their families.

With no work on the railways, Chinese men looked for other ways to earn money. They found work in the canneries, on the boats that sailed up and down the coast, and as servants in white households or hotels, but they were often paid less for the same work than non-Chinese workers. They set up small businesses such as market gardens, laundries, shops and restaurants. The city of Victoria had once had the largest Chinese settlement in Canada, but by the early part of the twentieth century Vancouver had surpassed it, developing a vibrant Chinatown with shops, theatres, newspapers, restaurants, tea houses and rooming houses, all serving the largely bachelor community of Chinese men in the area around Pender and Keefer Streets. Some Chinese men also left British Columbia, moving eastward across Canada in search of work.

Immigration from China continued, despite the head tax. During the last half of the nineteenth century and the early part of the twentieth century, China was in political turmoil as the Imperial system of government fell and warlords and politicians competed to take its place. Even additional increases in the head tax, and growing prejudice against Chinese, did little to discourage immigration — not even when, in 1903, the tax was raised to the huge sum of five hundred dollars.

An easy way to appreciate how much a burden this was is to realize that this would be the equivalent of nearly five thousand dollars in today's money. Mei-ling and her father would have had to save nearly ten thousand dollars to bring both her mother and brother to Canada if the head tax existed today. It's true that North America was regarded as "Gold Mountain" because the Chinese fared far better economically in Canada than they had in China, but they were still hard pressed because of sending money back home to their relatives.

Although Chinese men usually left their families in China, sending money home and visiting occasionally, some Chinese women did come to Canada. In 1861 Won Alexander Cumyow was the first Chinese baby born here. But women and families were always in the minority. The census of 1911 shows that, for every 10 Chinese women in Canada, there were 279 men. It was usually the wealthier merchants who brought their wives to settle in Canada, but for many poorer men this was the dream toward which they were working. Often, men would bring their younger male relatives or their sons first, because the men could work and help raise the money needed to bring over the women and children. Except in family-owned small businesses, there was no respectable work for women. Mei-ling's father, brought over by his uncle, fell into this category. Mei-ling's own situation, as a daughter brought to Canada before her mother, is a little unusual, but it is one that did occur occasionally.

As people realized that the Chinese community was here to stay, prejudice grew, often incited by reports in newspapers and pamphlets. In 1907 white rioters rampaged through Chinatown and the nearby Japanese area, breaking the windows of businesses. After the end of the First World War unemployment rose, and so did resentment of Chinese workers. They were accused of taking jobs away from white workers, and of being prepared to work for lower wages.

In response, the provincial government of British Columbia passed many laws which were designed to limit what Chinese workers could do, and how businesses they operated should be run. Chinese workers had not been allowed to vote in British Columbia since 1872. This excluded them from many professions, such as law, medicine and pharmacy, which required the practitioner to be on the electoral roll. In 1919 the Canadian government denied Chinese immigrants the right to vote at a federal level.

In 1922 the school board in Victoria, British Columbia, attempted to remove Chinese students from regular schools and place them in special classes. This was met with organized resistance from the Chinese community in Victoria, which boycotted the schools until this ruling was changed.

The Chinese were the only immigrant group to be targeted so specifically by legislation in this way, although during both world wars immigrants from countries at war with Canada —

such as Ukrainians and Germans in World War I, and Japanese in World War II — were forced into internment camps.

In 1923, what had long been feared by Canada's Chinese community came to pass. An act was introduced into the federal Parliament which would effectively end Chinese immigration, apart from very select groups such as diplomats and some students. The Chinese community rallied to fight this proposed legislation, but in the short time that it took the bill to be hurried through the House of Commons — from March to May of 1923 — their efforts were not successful. After passing through the Senate, the Chinese Immigration Act, commonly known as the Exclusion Act, became law on Dominion Day, July 1, 1923. For years afterward this day was known to many Chinese as Humiliation Day.

The Exclusion Act was a devastating blow for Chinese already living in Canada. Many men chose to return to China rather than face being separated from their families forever. Others remained in Canada, visiting their families when they could. This became more difficult after Japan invaded China in 1935, and even more so during World War II. There were many cases of husbands and wives who did not see each other for twenty years, and of fathers who never saw the children they had fathered on visits home until those children were adults.

The period after the introduction of the Exclusion Act has been described as an era of stagnation for the Chinatowns that had grown up across Canada. During World War II Chinese Canadians were very active in raising money for the war effort, and many young Chinese Canadians served in the armed forces, especially in Asia. After the war, the Chinese community redoubled its efforts to have the Immigration Act of 1923 repealed, finally succeeding in 1947.

Even after the Exclusion Act was repealed, however, it still took many years for families to be reunited, as the regulations affecting Chinese immigration remained quite strict. Families were forced to prove their relationships, which was difficult to do since many documents had been lost or destroyed during the war. Only in the middle of the 1960s were these constraints relaxed. This freer immigration policy has led to the vibrant Chinese community which is so much a part of Canada today.

*Thousands of Chinese men lived in camps such as this while working on the Fraser Canyon section of the Canadian Pacific Railway.*

*Once the railway work was finished in 1885, Andrew Onderdonk, the contractor, dismissed his crews. Many Chinese workers scrambled to find even low-paying jobs.*

*Living conditions for most Chinese men were cramped and meagre.*

*Shops such as laundries and restaurants employed many Chinese workers. Others took positions as houseboys in white households.*

*The largely "bachelor" Chinese community centred around Pender and Keefer Streets. Many men did have families, but these were often back in China.*

*School children at the Kitsilano Public Library, 1922.*

Chinatowns existed in other North American cities as well. This fish merchant's daughter lived in San Francisco's Chinatown in the early 1900s.

Though most Chinese students could not afford higher education, Dr. Victoria Cheung graduated from the Faculty of Medicine at the University of Toronto in 1923, her studies having been paid for by the United Church.

*The daughter of a janitor sweeps the sidewalk outside the Board of Trade Building on Pender Street.*

*Woodward's Department Store on Hastings Street.*

*Schools such as this one in Victoria had large populations of Chinese students. An attempt in 1922 to put all such students into separate classes met with strong opposition from the Chinese community.*

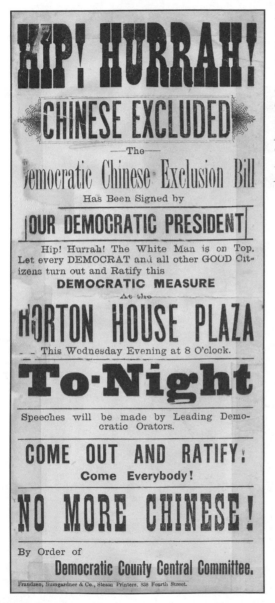

Many whites resented Chinese workers and were delighted with the passage of the Exclusion Act.

*The Head Tax certificate of Rhoda Chow, who came to Canada from Canton in 1913. Under the Chinese Immigration Act, the certificate cost her family $500.*

# Glossary

*Ai-yah* (i-yuh): all-purpose exclamation, used to express surprise, disgust, even joy

*Baba* (bah-bah): father

*cheong-sam* (chong-sam): dress

*Ching Ming* (ching ming): grave-sweeping day

*dim-sum* (dim-soom): various small savoury dumplings

*donggoo jinggai* (don-goo-jin-gai): steamed chicken with mushrooms

*Gum Shan* (goom-shan): Gold Mountain, the Chinese term for North America

*gwei lo* (gway-low): foreign devils

*jook*: rice gruel or porridge

*Kuomingtang* (kwo-ming-dang): nationalist party in China, now spelled *Guomindang*

*Kwangtung* (kwang-toong): now known as Guangdong province in China

*Oong choy*: Chinese pea vines

*maj joong* (mah-jong): traditional Chinese game played with domino-like tiles

*M'goi* (mmm-goy): thank you

*muui-jaai* (mu-ee-jai): bonded servant

*min-naap* (meen-nap): padded silk jacket

*mau-tin* (mao-din): small area of land, about 2/3 of a hectare or 1/6 of an acre

*Poon-yue* (poon-yoo-i): Mei's home county

*Toong Yuan* (toong-yun): rice-ball soup or family reunion

# Meanings of the Characters' Chinese Names

Chin Mei-ling 陈美玲
*Beautiful and clever*

Chin Wing-lok 陈永乐
*Always happy*

Chin Chung-yun (Baba) 陈重人
*Values people*

Chin Sing-wah 陈醒华
*Arise, China!*

Chin Lai-tsun (Ma) 陈丽珍
*Precious jewel*

Tsung Sook 钟 叔
*Uncle Tsung*

Wong Bak 黄 伯
*Senior Uncle Wong*

Yook Jieh 玉 姐
*Sister Jade*

Cheung Wan-sheung 陈雲湘
*Cloud River*

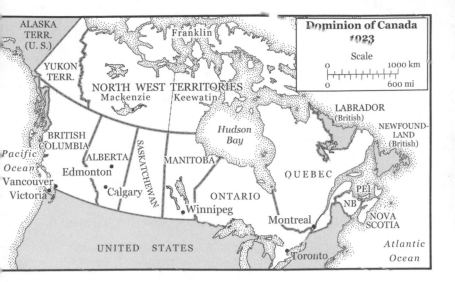

| Chinese population in 1920: | | | Total Chinese-speaking population in 2001 | |
|---|---|---|---|---|
| City | Men | Women | City | Population |
| Vancouver | 5,790 | 585 | Vancouver | 293,000 |
| Victoria | 2,938 | 503 | Victoria | 8,000 |
| Calgary | 649 | 39 | Calgary | 41,500 |
| Edmonton | 510 | 17 | Edmonton | 32,800 |
| Winnipeg | 790 | 24 | Winnipeg | 8,500 |
| Toronto | 2,019 | 115 | Toronto | 348,000 |
| Montreal | 1,628 | 107 | Montreal | 41,800 |

*Several Canadian cities (see map) had a significant Chinese population in 1923. Chinese men vastly outnumbered women in the 1920s, as shown in the table (above left) from the 1920 census. The Chinese-speaking population has dramatically increased since then, as shown in the table (above, right) from the 2001 census.*

# Acknowledgments

美

Grateful acknowledgment is made for permission to reprint the following:

Cover portrait: Detail (colourized) from black and white photo, DN-0005978, *Chicago Daily News* negatives collection. Courtesy of the Chicago Historical Society.
Cover background: Detail (colourized) from black and white photo, *Pender Street, ca. 1929*, Stuart Thomson photo, City of Vancouver Archives, CVA 99-2466.

Page 201 (upper): National Archives of Canada, Edouard G. Deville, C-016715.
Page 201 (lower): British Columbia Archives, B-03625.
Page 202 (upper): British Columbia Archives, D-00336.
Page 202 (lower): British Columbia Archives, F-00197.
Page 203 (upper): City of Vancouver Archives, DIST P168.1.
Page 203 (lower): Vancouver Public Library, 10442.
Page 204 (upper): Arnold Genthe, Library of Congress, FN 2332.
Page 204 (lower): Ontario Multicultural History Society.
Page 205 (upper): City of Vancouver Archives, CVA 99-1529, photographer: Stuart Thomson.
Page 205 (lower): City of Vancouver Archives, photographer: Philip T. Timms, CVA 677-611.
Page 206: British Columbia Archives, C-07921.
Page 207: British Columbia Archives, PDP03732.
Page 208: Courtesy of the Trail Historical Society.
Page 201: Chinese characters by Lu Yimin and Huang Wei.
Page 211: Map by Paul Heersink/Paperglyphs. Map data © 2002 Government of Canada with permission from Natural Resources Canada.

Thanks to Barbara Hehner for her careful checking of the manuscript, and to Dr. Anthony Chan of the University of Washington, author of such books as *Gold Mountain: The Chinese in the New World*, for sharing his expertise.

*For all those who came before*

Many people helped with the creation of this book and I would like to extend my thanks to all of them. In particular, I owe a huge debt to my husband, Henry Chan, who not only listened patiently as Mei's story unfolded, but who also was my translator, reading a whole year's worth of *The Chinese Times* on microfilm, allowing me to build up a picture of what life was like in Vancouver's Chinatown in 1923. In Vancouver, Larry Wong was a wonderful friend and resource, patiently listening to my endless questions and finding me the answers. The staff of Vancouver Public Library's Infoact service did a marvellous job pulling together many primary sources; this was of particular use in finding out what school life would have been like for Mei. In Toronto, Paul Yee was generous with his time and expertise, reassuring me when I thought I had written myself into a corner! Finally, my thanks go to Anne Sarndall, who is always my first reader.

— G.C.

# About the Author

美

Gillian Chan had a wandering childhood, "as my family moved every two years, following my RAF officer father, around England and Europe. Books were always very important to me because of this, providing me with something to do until I made new friends." Even today Gillian reads about four books a week — "more if I'm not writing, less if I am. I normally have a book on the go on each floor of the house." Books also gave her many ideas about what she wanted to do with her own life, including writing them herself. Another dream was to work in a field that allowed her to deal with the past, as history was always a passion. "I thought that I might like to be an archaeologist who wrote books about my discoveries."

After being a high school English teacher for ten years, Gillian realized her dream of becoming a writer in 1994. Her first book, *Golden Girl and Other Stories,* was short-listed for the Mr. Christie's Book Award. A companion collection, *Glory Days and Other Stories*, was also a Christie nominee, and made the shortlist for the 1996 Governor General's Award.

It was when she turned to writing novels that Gillian was finally able to combine her writing with her love of history. *The Carved Box*, her first novel, set in Upper Canada in 1801, grew out of her exploration of Canadian history. Having grown up in England, one of the first things that Gillian did after she and her husband moved to Canada in 1990 was read as much as she could about the lives of the early pioneers, marvelling at the hardships they had endured. Her next novel, *A Foreign Field*, sprang from her fascination with the period of World War II, but a new element was added as Gillian realized that her own uncle had trained in Canada during the war. "He became the inspiration for my main character, a young British pilot who lies about his age in order to enlist."

Gillian's husband is Chinese by birth and has many family members living in Canada. Listening to their stories of how and when they came to Canada led to Gillian's interest in the early history of Chinese immigrants to Canada. She became fascinated by how these immigrants overcame so many obstacles in order to make better lives for their families — obstacles that included prejudice, poor working conditions and legislation designed to limit their entry into the country. During her preparations for this book, Gillian travelled to Vancouver several times, walking the streets that would have been familiar to Mei. Her husband read and translated Chinese newspapers for her from the period in which the story was set, so that she could give an accurate picture of what life was like in Vancouver's Chinatown at that time.

Gillian's characters become very real to her — so much so that she often talks about them as if they are real people, and feels their sorrows and joys. "One day my husband and I were talking over dinner when our son came in and said, 'Why are you and Daddy so sad? Why are you crying, Mum?'" The answer: They were sad because of something that had happened to Mei!

**National Library of Canada Cataloguing in Publication**

Chan, Gillian
An ocean apart : the Gold Mountain diary of Chin Mei-ling /
Gillian Chan.

(Dear Canada)
ISBN 0-7791-1353-5

1. Chinese—Canada—Juvenile fiction. 2. Canada—Emigration and
immigration—Government policy—History—20th century—
Juvenile fiction. 3. Immigrants—Canada—Juvenile fiction.
4. Vancouver (B.C.)—History—Juvenile fiction. I. Title.
II. Series.

PS8555.H39243O34 2004      jC813'.54      C2003-904905-1

6  5  4  3  2  1  Printed in Canada  04  05  06  07  08

The display type was set in Phaistos.
The text was set in Tiffany and Humana.

美

First printing January 2004

*Alone in an Untamed Land*
*The* Filles du Roi *Diary of Hélène St. Onge*
by Maxine Trottier

*Brothers Far from Home*
*The World War I Diary of Eliza Bates*
by Jean Little